God's Hitman

Tales from the Lodge Vol 1

by "Doc" Clancy

CAVEMAN
ADVENTURE
LIBRARY
6

GOD'S HITMAN by "Doc" Clancy
TALES FROM THE LODGE VOL1
CAVEMAN ADVENTURE LIBRARY 6
First Printing, January 2023

Published by Quest Omnimedia, Santa Clarita CA
ISBN:979-8-9876309-0-7

PUBLICATION ORDER AND CREDITS

Hell Camino
***Bachelor Pad Magazine* #45, Fall 2018**

Outing to Nowhere
***Gnarly Magazine* #6, Fall 2018 and #7, Winter 2019**

Fire in My Head Blues
***Downbeat Drag* Vol 1 #6, Fall 2019 and #7, Winter 2019**

Ghost Town
***Pulp Modern* Vol 2 #5, Summer 2020**

Drive-Out
***CAVEMAN Magazine* #5, Winter 2021**

Goddess of Murder
***CAVEMAN Magazine* #6, Spring 2022**

Ain't No Grave
Previously Unpublished

The Valley and the Shadow
Previously Unpublished

COVER ART by Kevin Maginnis, from the original publication in *Gnarly Magazine*.

INTERIOR ART by Kevin Maginnis. Commissioned for this edition.

BOOK DESIGN and OOG LOGO by Michael Pfeifer

**For Yazmin,
who did not doubt.**

Foreword

I DIDN'T set out for this book to be as spiritual as it is. It's not that its religiosity lines up with my own beliefs, but there's a fascinating type of American Bible Christianity which though in practice is often intolerant and even dangerous, is at its best intense, deeply personal, and—as in the case of this book's central character, the gun-toting, psalm-quoting Rev. Xavier Holyoak—profoundly sincere.

Although we see the good reverend acquire items that I consider to be parts of his ongoing iconography—the '58 Bel Air and his Colt 45s specifically—I intentionally avoided making this collection an "origin story". Instead, we see the Rev. at various loosely connected points that probably take place near the beginning of his career as a hunter of dark things, or at least at the point where he is first becoming known and feared among the Children of the Devil.

The first story in this collection, "Ain't No Grave", is a new work written specifically for it, and allowed me to set the spiritual tone that makes these otherwise loose stories cohesive. It will surprise no one that I listened to a lot of latter-day Johnny Cash when writing it.

The first story written in this collection was "Hell Camino", based loosely on a joke that had circulated among my closest circle of friends. This was the first *Tales from the Lodge* story ever written, and the second to be published, *Bachelor Pad* beating out *Gnarly*'s "Outing to Nowhere" by only a few days. "Fire in My Head Blues" was written after these, as an attempt to go back and start establishing some of the mythology. This story took a while to find a home before ending up in *Downbeat Drag*, probably because it takes a lot for granted when read on its own. Though perhaps unsure alone, here it ties Holyoak deeply to his human failings.

"Ghost Town", appearing in the wonderful *Pulp Modern*, was a more confident take on a freestanding story and allowed me to introduce the Silver Sabremen—who are central to the *Tales from the Lodge* mythos—in the first published story to feature them prominently, with a cameo from the Terre Haute lodge's own Greg Hilsson.

By 2020 I was publishing my own magazine, with "Drive-Out" admittedly being written to fill a space. "Goddess of Murder" on the other hand, taking its name from a classic horror comic, had been on my mind for years prior, as the need for help identified in "Hell Camino" and the bridge from there to "Outing to Nowhere". It gave me the opportunity to enshrine the phrase "feral housewife" in English-language literature and is loosely inspired by a famous piece of kitsch pop art—but I'm not going to tell you which one.

Closing this volume is "The Valley and the Shadow", which started with my desire to have a unique villain that *Famous Monsters of Filmland* readers would have freaked out over and ended up being the work which ties all the scattered cords in this book together.

If you've been with me from the beginning, I appreciate your loyalty and hope you enjoy how I connected these loose ends. If you're a new reader, I hope you stick around: there's more where these came from.

-"DOC" CLANCY

Go tell that long-tonged liar,
Go tell that midnight rider,
Tell the rambler, the gambler, the backbiter,
Tell 'em that God's gonna cut 'em down.

-Traditional

Ain't No Grave

I

THE AIR outside was as cold as the whisky was warm. Xavier Holyoak had been staring at the bottom of that crystal glass for the last couple of hours, avoiding with limited success a chip in the rim. The chill outside was deep and cut to the bone as it crawled across the tavern's wooden floorboards—a bite that only the desert air could have at night was blowing in from land where the sun had already set. It was dark at the table in the corner of the bar, and a deepening purple was spreading across the sky outside.

If anyone had noticed his cleric's collar, they had elected to ignore it or at least remain silent. He longed to stay and sit a while longer, but the time was now. The Word was laying heavy in his chest and its weight increased with each moment that passed. There were monsters outside, and they needed the Name of Jesus.

A gasp went up from the painted women that drowsily marched between the saloon's few regulars. Holyoak looked up at the double swing doors and saw two eyes, burning red lights beneath a dirty Stetson. Like Jonah, he'd been in the belly of this bender for three days and like Jonah evading God's call, God had made other arrangements for their appointment.

He looked sideways across his shoulder, and the thing hissed almost silently between bared fangs that glistened in the twilight.

"Come on in," Holyoak said, turning back to his glass and draining it. The creature dashed over the doorway. Women screamed, men dove beneath their tables, the barkeep fumbled with a rifle under the counter. Holyoak rose and turned, raising a sawed-off shotgun at the slavering thing that charged towards him smelling of a lonely desert grave. He fired both barrels, lifting the creature from its feet, the momentum continuing to drag it outside after it touched the ground, leaving a streak of bright red, fresh blood with lines of black decay running through it.

The creature howled in the night as Holyoak stepped onto the saloon porch after it. It was clawing at its chest, which smoked from a hundred tiny wounds where rock salt, flakes of silver, and splinters from an old cross had entered its flesh. Throwing the smoking shotgun over his shoulder, Holyoak pulled a simple wooden cross from the pocket of his bomber jacket. His eyes focused on it for a moment. It gave him comfort. Then he watched as it drove the creature into a paralyzed rage.

"Where are the others?" he asked, but the creature was too old, too insane, or too injured to answer him.

"Right here, holy man," was the sneering response, far away down the street but as if whispered, spitting, in his ear. Down the street, eight figures stood. It was just after sunset and still light outside. Five males and three females, in what looked like fancy dress straight from the Old West.

Holyoak knew well that they could have closed the gap in a moment's bound, but they walked as if to a showdown. Holyoak sneered, drawing a stake from his coat and putting the creature at his feet out of its moaning misery. It was so old and brittle that he didn't even need a hammer, the stake piercing its ribs like a wasp's nest, and reducing it to dust and ashes at Holyoak's feet. He realized that the ache in his heart was gone: he was doing God's work.

"He killed Reg," a woman's voice said, dripping sweet poison.

"So might I have done—he was old and crazy," said a man's voice, effete, dry, and cold.

The first voice Holyoak had heard spoke up again: "But he was family, and the holy man will pay."

They were close to him now. With his lip curled in a hunter's cruel smile, Holyoak walked back over the threshold of the saloon.

"Oh," the leader of the pack snarled, stroking his beard beneath his wide, flat-brimmed hat. "Smart man. I'm gonna kill you so slow, Jesus is gonna get tired waiting up for you."

All around the room, patrons and barmaids were huddled, hidden behind the furniture, staring transfixed at the doorway. Holyoak had turned his back. He hoped he was strong enough but there was no point risking his soul. These people though were the weakest of sinners, addicted to the simplest of human failings. He thought this without judgment, only pity—and the knowledge of what a creature as powerful as the leader of this gang could do.

"Don't look!" One of the wenches had stood and was moving slowly towards the door, wide-eyed and unafraid. "Don't look at him!" Holyoak shouted again, pushing her roughly away, and turning to punch a besotted drunk that was attempting to get past, leaving him sprawling on the ground. He watched the figure in the doorway swivel his gaze from person to person, and he rushed to stop another man who could barely walk from stumbling over.

Too late he noticed a pretty girl who had been standing in the shadows in the corner nearest the door. She was young, probably new to the life she was living. She smiled, flashing her white teeth beneath her vacant, staring eyes. She curtsied. "Won't y'all please come in?"

Holyoak rushed to her, muscles straining. The creature broke his gaze on her, leaving her conscious and aware as he took her close and tore out her throat. She gasped silently, unable to scream as her blood sprayed all over the room. The monster's eyes were locked with Holyoak's the whole time, folding the girl in his arms, sucking and licking grotesquely, trying to capture as much of her rushing blood as he could in his mouth.

Holyoak was still, coiled like a spring. "You're going to die, God damn you." It wasn't a threat and it wasn't shouted or raged. Both parts of the sentence were statements of fact. Mechanically, as if of their own accord, he felt his fingers reload the shotgun.

"Been there," the creature smiled, it's mouth full of the blood that dripped down its bearded chin as it released the lifeless girl's body to the floor with a thud. "Done that." He stepped over her corpse, his disciples following, their shining, predatory eyes taking in every corner of the room, and every terrified face.

The bar's patrons scattered like frightened rats, blindly flailing for exits that didn't exist, a few that darted into the back room maybe escaping, but more likely cowering in false hope of safety until their murderers were done killing the rest.

"Judgment Day, holy man" their leader shouted, looking back at Holyoak as he tore the screaming barkeep limb from limb.

Holyoak tried to intervene, stepping between two barmaids and one of the females that lunged towards them, slavering. Her back was arched, her arms and legs stretched unnaturally, she looked like a wolf wearing the painted mask of a beautiful woman's face. And beautiful it was, despite the pale wild eyes and gnashing teeth, despite the crimson flow that dripped down her alabaster neck and heaving bosom. He understood how these creatures could fascinate people, even though to him the skin was too pale—no matter how lovely and feminine the shape, no matter how alluring and pulchritudinous her breast, it was a nest of vipers.

In an instant he raised the shotgun and fired both barrels again. The she-beast looked surprised as she was lifted off her feet, her beautiful bosom torn open like a ragged garment. As soon as she hit the ground, she flailed and raged at the smoke streaming from her torn body.

"Son of a bitch got Zelda!" one of the males shrieked. This had been a show of cruelty for his benefit, but they had counted on him being as terrified as the poor lost souls around him. The wolves had not counted on a dog among the sheep.

They were upon him in a swift movement of air. He heard the screams of the girls behind him—and the rabid howling of the creature he had laid low. He commended his soul to his God and the lights went out.

II

HOLYOAK AWOKE to a great pain in his arms and shoulders. He came to suddenly, awakened by the dove-like sigh of one of the two barmaids strung up next to him, the ones he had tried to save. Though he had half-expected to wake up at the Pearly Gates, the three of them were still alive, hanging from the ceiling of what looked like the saloon's wine cellar by their chafed wrists.

He smiled wryly to himself. Their hosts had something special in mind.

The door at the far end of the cellar slammed open, and a tall lean figure entered. This had been the leader's sidekick that had piped in during the initial fight. He had all the look of a dissolute, opium-addled dandy from a hundred years before. He wore an embroidered velvet vest, his black hair tousled carefully. His eyes were shot completely red and his skin was so white it was almost blue. His shaven chin was ruby red between his long sideburns.

"Zelda needs blood, holy man," he said, gripping Holyoak's face with an icy cold hand. His nails were long and carefully manicured, but yellow with the dirt of the grave. He grinned wolfishly. "You pick which one of them goes first."

The girls started struggling against their ropes, the girl on his left, the blonde, was weeping inconsolably. The brunette at his right was swearing like a sailor.

"Her," Holyoak breathed resentfully, indicating the brunette with a nod.

"You goddam son of a bitch cock—" the creature's hand over her mouth stopped the stream of vitriol directed at Holyoak as he dragged her away kicking and screaming and slammed the door behind them.

Holyoak strained his muscles, lifting his boots up above the rafter to take the weight off his wrists so he could untie the crude knot with his teeth. He dropped to the dirt floor silently and began untying the blonde. She began to cry out anew as he lowered her to ground, and he had to place a finger on her lips, his face almost against hers to keep her quiet.

He searched his pockets. "They took my gun, of course, and the stake." The cross was still there and he took it out, looking at it intently for a moment.

"You let them take Darlene," she said accusingly.

"Would you rather it had been you?" he asked, his eyes darting around the small room for implements. He picked up a creaky, rotten chair, and twisted it apart. "Hundreds of years old and they never think to clear the damn wooden furniture."

He snapped a chair leg into two sharp halves. "Be ready." He opened the door suddenly. Their guard was on alert, poised at the noise. He was shorter, less slim, rather nondescript except for his old-fashioned clothes and pale skin. He'd probably been a nobody in life and he wasn't quite the top dog in his crowd either. Holyoak's first thrust missed the heart by a few inches, resulting in a rush of blood from the creature's shocked, gaping mouth. The second was true, reducing him to a pile of bones and ashes as if his flesh had been blown away by a great South Wind. The frail stake was broken though.

She hung her head. "What are you gonna do?"

"More than one way to kill a vampire," he said.

"You mean, like getting them out in the sunlight?"

Holyoak shook his head. "That won't kill one unless they're very weak, though it'll slow 'em down and rob them of most of their powers."

They clambered up the stairs and into the main space of the saloon. Evidence of their captors' ferocity lay in the twisted and torn bodies and great streaks of blood along each of the walls and scattered among the tables and chairs. At the far end, a bloodsucker with a clean-shaven, blue face started. The thin leather strap of his cowboy hat dangled low beneath his chin, his crimsoned, gloved hands reached for them as his boots tramped with extra-human speed along the floorboards.

The girl ducked behind Holyoak.

"Here's one thing worth knowing," he said, flicking a wooden bowl of peanuts from the bar onto the floor. The vampire stopped in his tracks, eyes wide and darting at his feet. Holyoak flipped over all the remaining bowls within his reach.

"Vampires are all obsessives. They can't help it—it's part of the curse." He coaxed the shaking blonde from behind him to his side so she could see. "Before he can take a shot at us," Holyoak said, confidently placing a hand at his hip, "he's gotta count every last one."

"That won't kill him though, will it?"

"No, and it won't take forever, not with the creature's uncanny speed and vision." Holyoak was looking around. "Most people," he continued, don't realize that a body of running water will do the trick." He spotted the huge whiskey cask to the side of the bar.

"It's no time for a drink, mister!" the blonde shouted.

"This rotgut's so watered down, it ought to work." He looked around for something to break the spigot with, and spotted his shotgun nearby on the floor. He glanced back at his foe as he picked it up, and seeing him nearly at the end of his counting, hunched over and crazed, realized he had better hurry. "And you'll call me 'reverend' or not at all." He sighed. "What do I call you?"

"Ginny."

"See, Ginny," he said, "in the Bible, it says that the Spirit of God moved over the waters—an unclean spirit can't."

"And what happens," Ginny asked, maybe getting the idea, "if the waters move in right under a—a unclean spirit?"

Holyoak smirked, and drove the butt of the shotgun down, snapping off the spigot and a large chunk of the weakened wood holding it. The watery, barely amber liquor sluiced across the floor as the vampire turned back to them in surprise, washing away the scattered peanuts and instantly melted boots and feet alike, carrying away a jellied clump of bone as the creature fell forward, its whole body likewise dissolving into muck as the "waters" washed over it.

"Well, eh, reverend, you sure seem to know a lot about these sumsbitches." Ginny was emboldened now, no longer hiding behind him. If he'd had any kind of weapon that would have done any good he would have given it to her, but there were the sounds of a struggle, the muffled crying out of a woman and the calm, spiteful cursing of something less than men. He stepped in front of her again and led the way to what served as the back office.

"How else do you kill 'em?" she asked excitedly.

"Decapitation, force-feeding garlic, tricking them into drinking from a corpse, and–"

Holyoak was at the door, and though she looked expectant, his attention was now on turning the knob silently. God knew they'd made enough noise getting there, but vampires could be very oblivious when they were feeding… or being cruel. He prayed it was still the latter as he swung the door open and braced himself in the doorway.

"Darlene!" Ginny shouted.

"Get these no-good, shit-kickin'–" cold fingers tried to stop her mouth and were promptly withdrawn as she bit them. She was suspended by her ankles over an old, rusty bucket. The dandy had got her strung up—presumably with some help from his moldering friends—a scruffy male and a female with pearls in her red hair—who watched from around the room. But even with his dagger in hand, he was having a hard time keeping her still enough for the bloodletting. His friends, amused, were snickering at his difficulties.

Holyoak drew the cross from beneath his coat, and the room full of monsters gasped, fangs out.

Outnumbered three-to-one, this was a standoff even with the Lord on his side. At least Darlene was safe for the moment, but her body was clearly strained from the struggle and from her current inverted position. Her hair was falling from its arrangement and her ample chest was heaving beneath her simple blouse. The hoop earrings she wore jangled as she tried to shake herself free.

Holyoak noticed a machete leaning against a table nearby, just out of reach. The immediate response to his slightest movement towards it confirmed that any change in his position would put the quivering girl behind him—or the intended victim in front of him—at risk for her life. He weighed his options in stillness for a moment.

"Ah, hell," he said, drawing back his arm and launching the wooden cross at the dandy. It struck him between the eyes, knocking him out like a boxer with a glass jaw going down for the count. His buddies tried to move in, but Holyoak had kicked the machete up from the ground, catching it and placing it with the shotgun to make a bigger cross in front of him.

Again, they recoiled in fear and disgust. The dandy arose, but Holyoak saw he was careful not to look directly at the makeshift cross. The plain wooden one had left a clear mark on his face anyhow.

"Idiots!" he shouted. He can't hurt you with that blade! It isn't consecrated!"

"Ah, but you're forgetting," Holyoak said, grinning. He lifted his chin and pointed back a thumb at the starched white collar beneath it.

"Heavenly Father," he said, closing his eyes. He could hear the low, animal growl of his enemies, and to his shame, he opened them again. "Bless this instrument, in Jesus' name. Amen."

"Amen," Ginny said reflexively from behind him.

Holyoak's predatory grin widened, and he broke the cross, brandishing the machete and the empty sawed-off like sword and shield. The first vampire seemed to have taken it as joke, his teeth were still bared and gnashing as his head and left arm flew from his flailing body.

There was no blood to speak of when you cut an undead corpse with a sanctified blade, just the faintest sizzle of burning flesh at it passed through.

The female jumped up the wall as she ran toward him. He struck her hard with butt of the shotgun, sending her spinning around and ending nonetheless gracefully in a crouch, from which she pounced at him anew, only to find Holyoak's blade in her side, cutting out a thick and steaming wedge of cold flesh. She stumbled a few steps before the blade separated her shoulders from her head, which rolled across the room, bouncing off the hindquarters of the cowering dandy.

"No," he pleaded, raising his hands. With a short clean blow, Holyoak took them off. He kneed the creature in the back, putting his boot on the back of his head and pressing his face into the wooden cross which still lay on the ground. The vampire screamed inhumanly over the sound of his own sizzling skin.

"Sit thou at my right hand," Holyoak said, pulling the dandy's head up now in a painful arch, his knee still in his back. "While I make thy enemies thy footstool." He sliced his throat with the machete, then drew it across again and again in slow, wide strokes. It cut through the creature's flesh and bones like a hot knife in butter, and it screamed for as long as it could make noise, clattering madly, clutching with its fresh stumps at the empty air in the blind terror of a thing that had thought it would live forever and knew from personal experience that things so much worse than oblivion awaited it.

At last, the final bit of flesh at the back of its neck cut loose, and Holyoak tossed its head to the other side of the room.

With Ginny's help, Holyoak cut Darlene down and stood her upright. She fell into him, her feet unsteady, and he caught the full feeling of her lush body—almost a prime sacrifice—pressed against his. Her blouse was low, and the valley between her breasts was even more tantalizing viewed from the right side up.

She slapped him.

"That's for picking me to die first."

She slapped him again.

"That's for the way you're staring down my neckline just now."

She slapped him a third time.

"I don't know what that's for, but I'm sure you'll do something."

She raised her arm again, but he seized it in a gentle but very firm grip. His own palm felt rough against the silk of her skin.

"Why'd you go and pick me anyhow?" she looked at him, still reprovingly, but somewhat cowed.

"You were the tougher one. You'd last the precious few extra seconds I needed to get down here." She couldn't be too angry with that answer, and gloated before her blonde companion, who appeared dejected to know the truth.

"Well," Ginny whined, "I made it all the way down here, and rescued you too, didn't I?"

"Don't worry Ginny," Holyoak breathed. "There'll be time to show you're brave yet—there's still three of them, if you count Zelda, and we might as well. As long she isn't completely dead we don't know what she's got up her sleeve. And don't forget, their leader is one of the ones still kicking."

"Should we stay here?" Ginny asked, timid again.

"Definitely not," Holyoak said, hoping he didn't sound too contemptuous. "Look, they can move faster and more quietly than we can. It might not seem like it, but you're both safer where I can see you." He lit a gas lantern that he found in a corner of the room, pocketing the matches he found with it, and gave the lamp to Darlene. It was the dead of night now, and the whole place was dark.

Holyoak moved cautiously back out into the main saloon floor, then up the creaking stairs to the guests' rooms, the girls cautiously in tow. Ginny looked like she was frozen stiff, but her legs kept moving—she was more afraid of being left alone now then of following him into the monster's lair.

He kicked open the first door, brandishing his machete-and-shotgun cross, Darlene holding the lamp as high as she could. It was empty. At the second door, his chances were 2-to-1, but he kicked it open with the same rapid resolve. It was empty as well. There was only one door left.

He positioned the girls flat against the wall, and with a deep breath and a wordless prayer, he kicked open the last door.

"Just in time, holy man." The leader was there, on the other side of a bed with a worn and dirty blanket on which lay the supine form of the female, Zelda. She was pale, even for her kind. Her bodice was torn open—along with the dead flesh beneath it—and the unnaturally lush breasts poised above the tangled mass of jellied guts made her look every bit the image of Sin itself. She was frothing at the mouth and her eyes were cloudy. He expected her to be breathing wildly, but remembered that vampires only took in air to speak. A human would never survive in her state, and it didn't look like a vampire could for very long either.

The last female was there at his side as well. "And he brought snacks." She smiled, her silver eyes cold, her fangs hanging low below her thin lips. She had probably not been beautiful in life, the curse bringing its dark beauty out in her along with the worst of her hatred and murderous rage.

These two flinched slightly at the cross when he entered the room, and they were glaring at it now. These were the strong ones.

Once again, both he and his enemies were unable to move, locked in stalemate.

"Ginny," Holyoak began. "You remember what I was telling you before?"

"I think so," came the timid reply.

"Fire," Holyoak said flatly.

There was a high-pitched scream. It was Ginny, who had quickly pulled the lamp away from her friend and pitched it into wooden floor. It exploded in a pool of liquid flame, quickly catching the piles of dirty clothes and the hanging edge of the filthy bedspread. Terrified, the other female backed away as Zelda burst, seemingly unaware, into flame. The leader of the gang merely stared him down, the firelight flickering in his face.

"Out! Now!" Holyoak shouted, backing away with the cross before him, all the way down the stairs.

"Get outta here!" he shouted again over the growing roar of the flames.

Alone, the leader of the gang was coming down the stairs after him, gliding in a loop of smoke. The girls finally ran away, back out into the dark street. The horrifying screams of the last female vampire could be heard upstairs, but the leader moved stolidly towards him, across the floor now, the back of his coat burning with a low blue flame. Half turning to smoke himself, the vampire closed the gap, swiping aside the cross in a rage. The sawed-off shotgun rattled to the floor, but he was able to maintain a grip on the machete, even though caught off balance.

The screaming upstairs had stopped.

The platform that led to the rooms was buckling in the fire that engulfed it, and the railing fell down, carrying the flames with it into the pool of whisky that had by now mixed with the remains of the vampire they had mostly dissolved.

Holyoak knew he had to last just a few seconds—if he was killed quickly his foe would rush out and murder the girls next, before continuing his terrorizing of the whole town. The vampire swiped him aside, sawdust and splinters biting his face as he tried to roll over and right himself.

The creature picked him up, its fetid breath filling is nose and mouth. The flames had almost made it to the bar.

"Do you think Zelda suffered much?" Holyoak asked.

The creature bellowed its rage, launching him back against the far wall and sliding through the air in a cloud of smoke to hold him against it.

"Don't worry," Holyoak said, smiling painfully though his swollen mouth. "You'll see her soon."

The flames picked up as they touched the great barrel behind the bar, and the creature turned—too late, dropping Holyoak, who ran, his boots loud against the wooden floor. He was only a few steps from the door when it happened.

He didn't hear it so much as the absence of sound. A shock so great that he felt like he'd been struck by an angel, sounding the whole drum of his body and scrambling his organs. He had a new respect for Jacob.

He didn't even feel the fire at first, licking at his legs and back as he exited the burning saloon. He fell into the dirt road and kept crawling. He heard the shuffle of people running to help and straining to look up saw the girls huddled together, wide-eyed and terrified at his appearance. Then he sank into darkness.

III

THE COFFINS, most of them plain, unsanded pine, were lined up outside the town's little white church. Holyoak didn't know how many, and he was careful not to look too closely because he didn't want to know.

"Quite a motley judgment day," said a low, voice, masculine and powerful, but sweet as a bell. The town's pastor was a tall Black man, whom he knew only as Brother Isaiah. He was not wide of build like Holyoak, but with a powerful strength that one could tell was more than his presence or his faith. He dressed all in dull black, with a white collar and shiny shoes, and the thin ring of hair around his balding head made him look like a monk.

He was quite blind behind his dark glasses, but so adept that it was easy to forget.

He was referring to the fact that many of the bodies had been so badly ripped apart that the undertaker had been forced to do a lot of guesswork keeping like parts with like. Many of the coffins contained mere jumbles of flesh and bone and they were all closed for a reason.

"When the Lord comes," Holyoak breathed, his voice course in his throat, "he will know who is who."

"Amen, Brother Xavier," Isaiah looked out towards an old, abandoned field at the edge of town. You couldn't see it from where they stood, but few in this town would ever forget that it was there. "Do you think you got them all?"

They had gathered all the remains of the vampires that they could find there in that field after the fire, burned them again, drowned the ashes in water from the river where Isaiah baptized, buried the ashes in a silver urn, and salted the earth. But just like their human victims, there wasn't a lot left.

"I can't be sure," Holyoak said, somewhat truthfully. He was sure that he had—or wanted to be sure. It had been two weeks without occurrence, but the Lord had not commanded him to move on.

That wasn't a good sign.

"Lord willing," Isaiah sighed, rubbing his smooth head wearily, "we won't learn differently anytime soon."

Isaiah moved up the stairs into the church, and Holyoak followed. His legs and lower back had been pretty badly burned and it still hurt to walk.

There were only a few people inside. Some were probably still afraid to come out, even in the daytime. Others couldn't be dragged to a church from their gin-soaked hovels even to mourn a fallen family member or friend.

As they approached the pulpit, Holyoak looked around. Often, he was called in to places like this: people would be oppressed by some evil thing and they would reach out to him for help. Other times his own investigations would lead him into the path of something that needed to be put down, and sometimes, the Lord would somehow point the way and he would find himself in a place like this, with people who stared at him uncomprehending as they would at a dangerous stranger, or at best, a terrible, blood-soaked angel.

"Do you know what the difference is between you and the rotting corpses out there in those boxes?" Isaiah asked his meager congregation. There was uncomfortable silence in response. "The only difference," he continued, "is that you still have time to turn to Lord—time to repent your sins and change your life to live like God wants you to."

It was fairly rote stuff, and Holyoak watched the crowd for any kind of reaction, not finding any except for Ginny and Darlene making doe eyes at him from one side of the pews.

"For them," Isaiah continued, shaking his head, "there's no more time. They went to judgement, cut off in the blossoms of their sin, sent to account, with all their imperfections on their heads and on their souls." He went on like this for a while. He was hitting all the right notes, emphasizing words like *sin*, *Lord*, *God*. But this hardly seemed the crowd.

Holyoak was asked to do the reading, and he stood at the pulpit, drawing the worn and dogeared book of psalms from his pocket. He selected Psalm 51:

> PURGE ME WITH HYSSOP, AND I SHALL BE CLEAN: WASH ME, AND I SHALL BE WHITER THAN SNOW.
>
> MAKE ME TO HEAR JOY AND GLADNESS; THAT THE BONES WHICH THOU HAST BROKEN MAY REJOICE.
>
> HIDE THY FACE FROM MY SINS, AND BLOT OUT ALL MINE INIQUITIES.
>
> CREATE IN ME A CLEAN HEART, O GOD; AND RENEW A RIGHT SPIRIT WITHIN ME.
>
> CAST ME NOT AWAY FROM THY PRESENCE; AND TAKE NOT THY HOLY SPIRIT FROM ME.
>
> RESTORE UNTO ME THE JOY OF THY SALVATION; AND UPHOLD ME WITH THY FREE SPIRIT.

Isaiah cocked an eyebrow as he bowed his head, but nonetheless, joined in with the congregation's "amen" at the reading's end.

It was more of a reaction than anything in his sermon had provoked.

It took the rest of the afternoon and into early evening to finish the last of the burials. They had done the digging themselves, to spare the townsfolk the sight of the final preparations that would prevent their loved dead from changing into something else. They had done the work in solemn silence, but now, as they both leaned on their shovels, sitting on old tombstones and wiping the sweat from their brows, Holyoak spoke up.

"The *Hamlet* was a nice touch," he smirked.

"Not just Shakespeare, you know," Isaiah gleamed "I've slipped in Poe, Hawthorn, last week some Dante. These people barely know the Bible, let alone anything else. Half think I get it from the Good Book, the other half think I've got a honeyed tongue." He rested a moment on his shovel, smiling. "I read like it was going out of style when I could see."

"Well," Holyoak considered, "whatever brings them closer to the Lord."

"About that, Brother Xavier," Isaiah continued seriously. "I take it from your choice of reading that you disagreed with my sermon."

"No," Holyoak weighed his words cautiously. "I don't disagree—"

"A funny thing," Isaiah interrupted, with more than a hint of tension, "for a man wielding guns and knives in God's name to talk about His forgiveness."

"I do as He commands," Holyoak said defensively. "And…" the heat in his words was backing down. "In my journeys I've come to see—or believe anyway—that the Good Lord cares more about what we do with our hearts then with our bodies."

"Is that the kind of old-time religion you've been teaching those girls since you got here?" He was of course, speaking of the time he had been spending with Darlene and Ginny—at their insistence. They swore that hearing him read the psalms was an incitement to religious fervor.

Holyoak didn't answer.

"'Behold, I send my messenger before thy face, which shall prepare thy way before thee. The voice of one crying in the wilderness, prepare ye the way of the Lord, make his paths straight.'"

Isaiah intoned the worlds solemnly, "looking" at him, his physical eyes useless behind his dark lenses, but his soul staring deep into his. "I'm willing to bet," he said after a moment, "that there was a time—and perhaps that time is now—when you believed that those words were written about you."

Holyoak's glare smoldered, unseen by Isaiah like the sun beating down on the oblivious mountains.

"Don't be offended," Isaiah relaxed and smiled again. "There was a time surely, when I thought they were all about me. See," he held up a hand, and Holyoak realized he had not seen the knotty scars there before. "I was once on a quest like yours. This isn't the first time I've seen these kind of monsters, though I had believed that long ago had been the last. My mission from the Lord has ended but you…" he seemed again to be peering into Holyoak's soul. "…yours is only just beginning. There's no telling what God has in store for you."

All the toughness and meanness that had been coiling in Holyoak since this conversation began melted away, leaving him sunken and vulnerable. "When did you know?"

"Know what?" Isaiah asked, patiently.

"When God's plan for you was done."

"God's plan for us is never done, Brother Xavier," Isaiah smiled. "But I had asked Him to give me a sign," he removed his thick sunglasses, revealing the red scars that passed across his permanently sealed eyelids, "and I knew that He was finished with that part of my life when He took my eyes."

IV

HOLYOAK WAS walking to the little boarding house where Ginny and Darlene lived together. The night was still and quiet except for a few lazily moving folks and the creaking of crickets between the streetlamps.

He had been spending a bit of time there. But he would have spent the time reading from his book of psalms anyway, and it was good for a man of God to preach from the Good Book once in a while between steps in whatever thankless quest the Lord had placed him on.

It was all tame anyway: he pretended not to see the way they made eyes at him while he read, apparently unaffected by jealousy between them, and they pretended to be rapt in attention at his rather uninspired but earnest recitation of his favorite works of David.

It was better that it was always the two of them together, he thought. *Or maybe,* he reflected, realizing that his face was twisting into a rather boyish, knowing smile, as he tugged nervously at his collar, *it's much, much worse.*

It was at that exact moment that the darkness flooded in.

He awoke laying on his back. Rough, splintered wood was chafing at the burned and tender backs of his legs through his pants. His dim and blurry vision focused on a figure in a wide brimmed hat standing above him in a narrow patch of light.

"There you are, holy man," spat the leader of the vampires he had slaughtered. One side of his face was burned and healed over like a candle that had melted and cooled. His beard was singed away in places and looked dark and crispy where it stood. His eyes glinted red in the light of the torch which danced before him, cruelly mocking his wounded visage.

"You almost missed your own funeral."

He squatted on his heels to get just that much closer. "You killed my whole little tribe," he said coldly. "You know something," the vampire said, grimacing. "Not my ma, not my pa, not my nigra-loving army sergeant back in '63: I ain't never hated anybody as much as you. Now they all got knives in the back. I liked that when I was human—sharp and cold and clean, with just enough time to see who done ya. But I got something special planned for you."

Awareness was finally dawning on Holyoak. He was realizing where he was and what was happening, but he was still stunned. He reached into his pocket but couldn't find any of his weapons—not even the little wooden cross.

"Good night, holy man," the creature said, waving its long-nailed fingers to command the lid of the coffin down. Holyoak heard and felt the impact of the nails sealing it shut with unnatural speed, followed by the animal efficiency of the dirt being burrowed back over what was meant to be his last earthly abode.

His resolve broke and he cried out, something between a scream and a panicked choke. Frantically, he tested the limits of the coffin with his limbs, crying out again and cursing. Then he was alone, in silence and darkness.

The beating of his heart slowed in his ears, the ragged breath became calm.

He felt that ache in his soul that he always felt when God commanded him to go on. For a moment he stared in the dark at a coffin lid that he knew was a few inches away even if he couldn't see. But the commandment only grew clearer.

"Here I am, Lord!" he shouted aloud. He felt he had gained an insight as to what it would be like when Gabriel sounded his horn and the dead awoke in their graves. And he was convinced of the fact that if God had sounded the call, then God would clear the way.

IT TOOK him the better part of a day and a half before his raw, torn hands felt the open air, another day and a half in a stupor of lights and noises before he came to his senses, laying in a plain bed in the house in back of Brother Isaiah's church.

It had been conviction first, then instinct, then something akin to madness as he clawed his way back to life, and then a long walk of the soul to reunite his human mind with the broken thing that had crawled out of that narrow hole.

It would not have been possible to define the moment he was first conscious and aware again—it came in phases and went again as quickly. Isaiah had nursed him, spoon-feeding him water at first, then broth and then hearty stew with wild herbs.

It became clear that the preacher was holding something back, but for a time Holyoak was too weary to speak, let alone ask questions. Then finally he started up.

"The vampire!" he shouted. "There's one left! The leader, he–"

"Yes," Isaiah said, setting the wooden bowl on the nightstand. "A lot has happened–"

"While I've been lying here!" Holyoak swung his legs out to stand up but was weak from the effort and slumped into the bed again. "How– how long."

"Three days, about," Isaiah said rubbing his bald pate. "Including your time in the ground—very biblical of you, by the way."

Holyoak tried to laugh, but only produced a dry croak. "I– hesitated when I arrived here. Three days. Unsure of where to begin. Not trusting that the Lord would show me…"

"Then the scales are even again, Brother Xavier."

Holyoak held this in his heart and found it to be true. God had not punished him. Only reset the balance of their covenant.

Isaiah sighed deeply, letting his head droop.

"These have been eventful days. Your foe walks again, feeding at will like a wolf among *my* sheep, and I, powerless to challenge him."

"How many victims?" Holyoak said through gritted teeth.

"Many sick." Isaiah was holding back again but felt Holyoak's insistence in a strong grip on his arm. "Only two dead so far."

"Who?" Holyoak squeezed tighter, afraid of the answer.

"You'll see for yourself soon." He lifted his head, breathing deeply to catch the smells of the darkening air outside. "Almost nightfall now." Holyoak relaxed his grip, but now it was Isaiah's turn, clutching at his shoulder.

"We went to bury them this morning, but they weren't at the undertakers anymore," Isaiah was a little frantic as he spoke. A chill crept into the room from the window, like the feeling you get in a fog. The light was foggy too, as if the room had become damp, but there was no visible mist, just the sensation of it.

"Don't look!" Isaiah shouted, knowing it was meaningless.

Holyoak turned to the window behind them slowly, the hair at the back of his neck standing up with a rigid, electric tingle. Ginny and Darlene were there, bathed in the moonlight which lit their pale flesh and savage eyes with its own brand of milky luminescence. They were floating in the space of the window, a little above the ground, their hair and their fanciest dresses—the ones they had been buried in—blowing in the strange billows of unfelt winds.

"Read to us," Ginny cooed.

"Pray with us, reverend," Darlene sighed.

They smiled sweetly, seductively, their grins dominated by long, shiny, new fangs.

What little strength Holyoak had was all in his clenched jaws and trembling fists.

Isaiah released his hold as he felt Holyoak's resistance wane. "What are you doing?" he asked.

"I will say of the Lord, He is my refuge and my fortress: my God; in Him will I trust.

"Surely he shall deliver thee from the snare of the fowler, and from the noisome pestilence…" Holyoak kept his head bowed, eyes closed in silent prayer for the rest of that night. Isaiah kept his hand upon his brother's shoulder, giving what he could of his own strength to the supplication.

And the girls watched, and waited, smiling at the two men of God who ignored their presence, as patient as the ages, until the first light of dawn.

"Now," Holyoak said, rising. "And quickly."

Without being told, Isaiah gathered the shotgun, the machete, and the wooden cross and put them in Holyoak's hands as he found the place for each one. Then he gathered up two rusted shovels, a hammer, and a pair of simple garden stakes and followed Holyoak outside. They moved into the pale light following the bilious forms of the two dead girls as they retreated backwards, still facing them, their feet never touching the earth.

The psalm still rang in Holyoak's head:

He shall cover thee with his feathers, and under his wings shalt thou trust: his truth shall be thy shield and buckler.

A vampire left little by way of spoor, but they had the high ground, and Holyoak could see clearly the path they took down the hill into a small rocky valley beyond.

Thou shalt not be afraid for the terror by night; nor for the arrow that flieth by day; Nor for the pestilence that walketh in darkness; nor for the destruction that wasteth at noonday.

It was a patch of freshly turned earth that they saw them enter at last, almost concealed from the town, sitting in the shadow of a derelict old mansion far off on the plain. A great, shallow hole had been dug here, and two open coffins, aged and mildewed, lay exposed to first rays of morning light.

The girls settled back into them as no living thing could, and as the coffins closed, the earth folded over them like children wrapping themselves in a blanket.

A thousand shall fall at thy side, and ten thousand at thy right hand; but it shall not come nigh thee. Only with thine eyes shalt thou behold and see the reward of the wicked.

Isaiah and Holyoak moved together seamlessly. Isaiah's muscles seemed to be remembering an old task, and Holyoak did not need to tell him to dig. The dirt was soft and damp with desert dew, and the coffins were not buried deep. They opened the first, Ginny's, and Holyoak was given pause.

Because thou hast made the Lord, which is my refuge, even the most High, thy habitation; There shall no evil befall thee, neither shall any plague come nigh thy dwelling.

He had not previously felt vulnerable to any undead thing's charms, but she appeared lovelier, more innocent, more vulnerable than ever she had in life. *Appeared* he reminded himself, steeling his nerve for the task.

Isaiah set the crude stake in his palm, and their hands touched for a moment, human warmth to human warmth. Holyoak moved closer to the coffin, climbing down into the dirt beside it. He placed the stake over her heart and the flesh that touched his hand was cold—not even the clammy cold of a dead thing, but the empty cold of glass or stone. Isaiah passed him the hammer, and he brought it down.

He shall give his angels charge over thee, to keep thee in all thy ways. They shall bear thee up in their hands, lest thou dash thy foot against a stone.

Blood shot like a geyser from the chest of the thing that had been Ginny. She opened her eyes, shrieking, and a second shriek, stifled by the other nearby coffin answered, the wooden box rocking with tumultuous movement. Holyoak brought the hammer down again and there was stillness. Ginny smiled, like a human being again, eyes closed in peace, and he groaned in relieved disgust as he drew the blessed machete from his side and severed her head in one clean blow.

Thou shalt tread upon the lion and adder: the young lion and the dragon shalt thou trample under feet.

They moved cautiously to the second coffin. It was still again and quiet, but Holyoak kicked it open, brandishing the little cross from his pocket before him. Darlene was awake and waiting, but the sun was up, and she lay torpid, a newborn thing only safe from being burned alive in its light by the narrow shadow of her fresh tomb. She stared aghast at the cross and flinched when Isaiah by instinct alone placed the stake over her heart. Holyoak brought it down with a horrible shout, this time driving the steak clear through her body and into the rotted wood beneath her back with one clean blow.

Because he hath set his love upon me, therefore will I deliver him: I will set him on high, because he hath known my name.

Her face in repose was perhaps not so angelic as her friend's but took on a look of great peace before Holyoak calmly severed head and body. The men of God rested a moment, panting and exhausted before reburying the bodies. They searched the area for any sign of the creature that had turned these girls and that still roamed free. They considered going to old ruin of a house further on, thinking it a good bet that this was the thing's home. But Holyoak thought better of it.

He shall call upon me, and I will answer him: I will be with him in trouble; I will deliver him, and honour him. With long life will I satisfy him, and shew him my salvation.

"There's no point. He'll be back in the town tonight. And I'll be ready for him."

VI

IT WAS a dark and clear night, dark enough for the moon to cast long shadows on the hard blue clay. Holyoak knew that the monster he hunted would be there tonight—he was not one to sulk at windowpanes.

Holyoak stood at one end of main street, sawed-off shotgun in one hand and sanctified steel blade in the other, like a ray of silver in the glow of the moon.

The monster stepped into the street at the other side, turning suddenly at the feeling of another presence—and one unafraid. He shook his head bitterly, and looked up, his eyes burning red in the black space beneath his wide hat.

"You just won't stay dead, will you holy man?" his voice seemed to reverberate through the whole valley in which the town lay, but the tone was subdued, frustrated even. He walked towards Holyoak, closing the gap quickly though it was a slow stride.

"That's okay," he said, stopping about twenty paces in front of him. Holyoak could see his long, sharp teeth set in a vicious smile. "Gives me the pleasure of killing you again."

They stood staring for a moment. Holyoak would not have been able to see his eyes if they didn't burn, unblinking and bright embers.

"Well," the vampire continued, "here we are: High moon." He laughed, a dry choking sound. He seemed to think that was especially funny.

Holyoak took in the scene. It was actually closer to twenty-five paces between them. His sawed-off would be casting a pretty wide spray at that range. The burned down saloon was down the street, closer to his opponent, the church was almost exactly between them. The moon had a great ring in the sky around it and illuminated thick and heavy clouds that stretched from horizon to horizon. There was a cold wind blowing in from the desert, and it carried the gentle promise of the smell of rain.

The street was gradually growing darker as those clouds moved between the ground and the moon. There was rain visible in the distance, out in the desert.

The vampire pointed to the iron T atop the church steeple. Holyoak noticed that he didn't flinch. "I'm gonna nail you to that cross," he stated flatly through gritted teeth, "so you've got a nice view of what I do to this town."

Lightning lit the distant mountains, sounding like a low rumble a few seconds later.

"Shame about the girls," he continued, having failed to produce any more of a response than the wind in Holyoak's hair. "They would have been good brides." He smiled even wider, even meaner. "I'm sure it hurt you, to put 'em down. Their blood was gooood, though."

Holyoak was past anger now. He stood in conviction and righteousness. He would not be moved.

The rain started then. A few scattered drops that Holyoak would have barely noticed if not for the hissing sound they made when they fell on the vampire, who ran, lumbering at first before picking up speed. Holyoak watched closely, bracing the stock of the shotgun at his elbow, and fired at the first moment that he knew the creature's body would catch most of the shot.

The monster turned to a figure of smoke at the instant he pulled the trigger on both barrels, the gray cloud continuing to roll towards him, parting in curls where the shot of salt and splinters passed through. There was still the impression of a man's shape at the center of it, still the hateful face and the wide-brimmed hat, and where the charge hit there, it chipped at the surface leaving bloody scabs on its face and in its chest. But the cloud solidified again toe-to-toe, picking Holyoak up by the throat and sending him crashing into the hard dirt street.

The vampire roared like a lion, hunched over, fangs out like a beast about to strike, its eyes very nearly ablaze. If anything, the blow Holyoak landed had not only enraged it, but given it more size and power from its rage. The rain was coming down harder now, and streams of smoke and steam rose from the vampire's body, the water cutting clean and bloodless furrows in its flesh.

This one really was old and strong.

Holyoak tried to block a furious blow with the shotgun, only to have it tossed aside like a toy.

He parried the next blow with the blessed machete, sinking it deep into the monster's wrist. A gooey clump of blood oozed around the blade, but the creature was undeterred, pressing his full weight upon him, even against the razor-sharp sword in its arm. Holyoak was off balance, his back strained at a painful arch, being pressed down into the mud.

Holyoak began to pray. He closed his eyes. The creature raged and roared. But Holyoak was speaking to his God and was not disturbed.

This time, he did not doubt.

"Show me the way, Lord. Guide my hand to do your work."

When Holyoak opened his eyes, he noticed something moving in the dark atop the roof of the church, a flash of nearer lightning showed it to be Isaiah. He was moving like a man led by unseen hands, impervious to the rain and to his own blindness. He had climbed the steeple now and appeared to be shaking the cross loose from the old and weakened wood that held it.

Holyoak shouldn't have known what would have led Isaiah to do such a thing, but they were men cut from the same cloth, and he knew what it was like to be commanded from on high. Neither of them had to understand—but he thought now that he did.

Summoning the very depths of his strength, he forced his way back onto his feet, the vampire at last wrenching his wrist free of the blade, exposing a deep and very wide chunk that had had been removed from his flesh and which was filling with gelatinous gore. Holyoak took the offensive, pushing his foe back further and further towards the church. He didn't dare risk alerting his enemy to their plan by looking up, but the cross was loose enough now to be visibly rocking in his peripheral vision.

The creature was stunned by his ferocity, blocking repeated blows with the sanctified weapon, his arms becoming covered with cuts even through the thick coat that he wore. They were in front of the door to the church now, but Holyoak knew as soon as he stepped clear, the creature would instantly close any gap between them. His muscles straining, his faith and resolve pushed to the limit, he gained a few precious feet.

Lightning struck, but at the same instant he heard the wood at the top of the steeple crack. The vampire should have heard it too, but it was drowning in its own fury. Holyoak stopped his assault, rapidly taking three steps back, trying to keep his balance at the sudden shift in movement. The vampire snarled, leaping towards him at the exact moment that the cross came down.

Lightning struck again, closer this time. The shape of the vampire, hunched over, his hat knocked off and his long hair wet with rain was visible. His skin crackled and hissed in the rain and his eyes had become dull as hot ashes. The long arm of the cross was through his chest, and twin streams of black and red blood flowed slowly down his body, mixing with the smoke and the rain.

He started laughing.

His eyes flared red hot again. He took a great step towards Holyoak, who slipped, falling in the slick mud of the street with just enough strength left to climb onto the wooden porch of the church.

"Where is your God now, holy man?" the creature spat.

And the world was consumed with light. Holyoak was totally blinded by the sun that appeared before him, the crash that filled the heavens seemed louder than any heavenly trumpet.

It was the blackness of the shape at the center of the lightning that he saw first. The vampire, his long hair and beard gone, his skin withering, flames of fire shooting from his mouth and his eyes.

He collapsed at Holyoak's feet, stiff and still, a burned and smoking thing with the red-hot lightning rod of the cross still in its body. It looked up with a swollen but still very sentient eye, its twin burned out in a hollow socket. The gaze was full of impotent hate.

Holyoak raised his boot over that staring orb.

"God is not mocked," he said, and brought the boot down into a skull that gave way like wasp paper.

Isaiah had found his way down, and they stood in silence together, watching the ashes of the vampire wash away with the wind and rain, until only the cross remained.

Fire in My Head Blues

AS NEAR as he could tell, he was about twenty miles deep into the middle of nowhere. When the biggest town you'd seen all day was Asp Fork, Tennessee—which he was pretty sure most of the people in Tennessee had never heard of—you knew you were in trouble, especially with that needle in the dash so close to empty.

"It's the Kustom Kreeper here again boys and ghouls," a comically monstrous voice said from the radio. "I hope you're all enjoying yourselves in the dark toni–" Holyoak brusquely switched it off. He hadn't been able to get anything but this hackneyed host and his bizarre assortment of rock 'n' roll, blues, and country on the radio for miles and most of the songs seemed to be about monsters or murder anyway.

"Damn," he swore softly but aloud, then he saw the blessed letters G-A-S shine like a neon beacon. "And thank you, Lord."

He pulled into Bradford and parked beneath the sign. The opposite edge of town was in sight from here. He might have driven through and missed the whole thing were it not for that marker, and for the whole meager population seemingly huddled across the street in front of its hall. A uniformed man with thick whiskers and no front teeth, ran across the street. "Evening sir," the attendant said as he slid over to the beat-up old truck and began to fill the tank.

Holyoak nodded and began to make his way across the street. He was a broadly built man, and his heavy bomber jacket made him look even bigger. His face was handsome but marked with the hardness of the lives he had led. He pulled down the jacket's zipper and exposed the black shirt and white collar underneath. The people of the town were engaged in a heated discussion about something and only took notice as he came within the glow of the streetlights.

"Evening," he said extending a hand to the gray-suited, older gentlemen whose presence at the center of the agitation seemed to mark him as in charge. "I'm Rev. Holyoak, just passing through," he said. "What's got everybody out here in the middle of the night?"

"Oh I sure am glad you're here Reverend," a tall and very thin man said, excitedly taking Holyoak's offered hand and interrupting anything the man-in-charge might have had to say. "Wasn't I just saying, Mayor, that we need a preacher for this."

"Yes, you were, Lawrence Clay," the man-in-charge said, taking Holyoak's hand as soon as Clay released it. "Mayor Cook, Reverend," he said, but his words hung in the air.

"What's the trouble then?" Holyoak asked, impatiently.

The townspeople looked at each other. "Well, I wouldn't have you think us yokels," the mayor said. "We were just discussing some strange fires that Mr. Clay here *claims* to be seeing around his farm."

"I ain't claimed nothing," Clay stated flatly. "I done *seen* something. Little fires on my farmland, movin' around in the dark at night for more than a week. But nothing burned in the morning. I got brave the other night and went out to chase 'em down, but whatever was there ran off."

Holyoak knew the world was full of rational explanations. But he also knew there were plenty of evil things moving about in the dark. It was his business to know. And he'd heard similar reports in Asp Fork and in the tiny gas station-less villages between there and here, only they'd stopped after a night or two. Something was on the move—and it may have settled in here.

Most of the time he was called in for trouble like this. If there wasn't information, there were at least instructions. But when you didn't know anything you had to start somewhere: "Does this town have a library?" he asked. A library or the oldest, loneliest person in a town were usually the best starting points, and the library was usually run by the oldest, loneliest person in town.

"You'd want to be talking to Ms. Armstrong," the Mayor said, confused.

"Yes," a smoky voice responded from nearby. A head and well-tapered torso swiveled back towards them from atop the sturdiest-looking blue-jean clad hips and hindquarters Holyoak had seen for a long time. The lenses of her glasses were full of the electric light of the streetlamps, hiding her eyes, but her red-gold hair and flashing smile immediately dispelled the mental image of the wizened spinster that had entered his head when he heard the name.

"Reverend," the mayor said, "this is our town librarian, Mabel Armstrong."

"Pleased to meet you," Holyoak said, taking her small hand in his and hoping that she couldn't detect the way his eye had been roving over her body.

"And you, Reverend," she said with a playful smile and a bat of her long lashes that said that she had.

"What're we gonna do, Reverend?" Clay asked, exhibiting again his talent for cutting in as he drew a rather dowdy looking woman and a frail teenage boy that looked like a miniature version of himself closer.

"Nothing tonight," the mayor responded for him. "Reverend, there's a room in back of my store. I'll put you up there for the night."

"But–" Clay began again. Despite his inability to articulate, Holyoak saw a real fear there that mere superstition and ignorance could only ape.

"No buts, Lawrence," the mayor said, exasperation entering his tone. "This man is a visitor and a man of God. He's already offering to help but he needs his rest."

"I'm obliged to you," Holyoak said, as they walked toward the general store. The rest of the town was moving off and Holyoak did his best to ignore the Clay family watching him helplessly—or the way that Mabel lingered for a moment before heading home.

"Will it be alright, Pa?" he heard the junior Clay ask.

Holyoak stopped and turned around. "I'll do whatever I can, son," he said with a smile. The boy smiled back, and the Clays at last turned to go.

Holyoak spent the rest of the next morning in the library. Mabel did not allow him to smoke among the books, so instead he had been drinking coffee until he lost count of cups. By now, in the late afternoon, he could taste the bitter flavor behind his eyes and only continued to sip at it because Mabel continued to bring it, hanging around him like a perfume. He'd been through endless records and forests worth of newspaper but could only conclude that Bradford was a totally unremarkable town.

"Find anything?" Mabel asked from over his shoulder, with that voice like honeyed whiskey lingering hot-breathed at his ear. Her strawberry blond hair hung down around her face, her slim waist pivoted forward on that sturdy-built, country body, her glasses fallen to the tip of her nose and her blue-sky eyes peering over the top.

Only temptation, he thought to himself. He shook his head. Mabel rose up in a wide-armed stretch that seemed to start in her open-toe heels and end in the painted tips of her fingernails, pressing the ample curves of her body against her denim jeans and gingham shirt on the way. Holyoak felt an itch at his starched white collar and he turned his gaze back to the text before him.

"This is the most interesting thing I've found," he said, changing the subject away from her bounties. She of course, took this as an invitation to lean over his shoulder, her hand at the nape of his neck. "Apparently," he continued, clearing his throat, "Bradford used to be a stop on the old Blues circuit. There was an old music hall that burned down and from what I can tell," he moved a wrinkled and yellowing map in front of him, "it was located where the Clay farm is now."

"What's that?" Mabel asked suddenly. There was a commotion outside which was growing nearer. Holyoak stood abruptly and tramped to the door. The young junior Clay was walking up the main street alone with a small but growing crowd accumulating a short distance behind him. He was in a daze and was covered with blood. Mabel ran out to him, only to be stopped in her tracks by Holyoak's firm grasp.

"You don't know what's wrong with him," he said. She glared at him with such heat that he dropped her arm, but she nonetheless pulled it away for effect before marching out towards the Clay boy.

He stopped as she approached, but it took a moment for him to register her presence. He looked her in the eye and screamed, then fainted into the dust.

The scene was lit eerily through the planks of the old Clay farmhouse as Rev. Holyoak wheeled the old truck slowly through the dirt yard. Mabel had been insistent on going with him, so he had agreed to meet her at 2 AM, so they would have time—but not too much—before dawn. It was now 12:15. He was hoping his work would be done before she realized he was standing her up.

He parked a short distance from the house, keeping to the shadows. His boots ground against the dirt as he stepped down from the truck and bowed his head, focusing his strength, driving those thoughts away, and rededicating himself to his Lord. After a moment of silence, he reached behind the seat and produced the shotgun, running his hands over the worn stock. "Thy rod and Thy staff they comfort me," he said, his sincerity cut with a wry sense of the absurd, and laid the weapon across his shoulder.

He moved resolutely towards the farmhouse, pulling the heavy front of his bomber jacket close to his starched white collar and dropping the gun level before him as he approached the door. Little twangs of music became audible as he drew closer, and did not stop even when he kicked the door in.

He fired as he stepped into the house, both barrels in tight sequence, the buckshot clanging metallically as each pellet found purchase. Still the plucking sounds continued. At the far end of the room sat a man in an old but well pressed, brown pinstripe suit, with shiny, two-tone shoes. The backs of his hands were dark, but he saw blood on the pale palms and shiny fingernails, and smeared all over the guitar that he held in his hands. Holyoak had hit him both times, squarely in the face, but his whole head was made of solid, orange-hot metal, and some of the shot still clung to it, slowly melting in its heat.

As the smell of gunpowder faded from his nostrils, it was replaced by the unmistakable, rusty smell of blood, and Holyoak saw the pieces of the Clays strewn across the floor around the figure's feet. Only now did the random sounds coming from the instrument stop as the man with the burning head looked up.

"I jus' can't manage it," he said. His eyes were surprisingly human, considering that they were white heat at the center of a furnace, and his voice was rich and silky smooth. "I jus' can't play without Irene. And I been lookin' everywhere for her." Holyoak continued to be ignored as the being in front of him started playing again, this time hesitatingly catching the tune and playing again, more smoothly.

"Did you kill these people?" Holyoak demanded, sickness and regret coiling in his guts at not having saved them. He was still gripping the spent shotgun tightly.

"Oh, I didn't mean too, and anyway, I let their little one go," the man with the fiery head said. "I needed a gee-tar and this would have to do. Only I couldn't concentrate on my playin' with them screamin' and carryin' on." He shifted in his seat, and a lick of flame flicked from his head as he moved. "You see, the Ol' *Masser,*" he said bitterly, "he wants a new song, so I got to get him a new song." He ran his bloodstained fingers down the fretboard of the guitar, adding a new layer of crimson streaks. "But it ain't the same without Irene." Again there was white heat in his grin and his eyes as he said: "It's gonna be twice as hard and half as fast."

Holyoak was at a loss. The shotgun had not had any effect and he didn't have a plan B. "What are you?" Holyoak said as he straightened his spine. "In God's name…"

"Used to be everybody knew who I was," came the response with a searing, bright smile. "And that's not a name to be mentioning in my presence."

"The face of the Lord is against them that do evil, to cut off the remembrance of them from the earth." Holyoak opened the break of the gun and jerked it back to eject the smoking shells.

The random notes being played on the guitar had been gradually taking a shape that seemed almost familiar, and now was the beginnings of a tune. "See," the voice continued to pour velvety from that mouth of flame, "you're only proving my point. Ain't no Holy Ghost can write like this:

"There's a fire in my heart, girl and it burns there just for you,

But it's the fire in my head that always tell me what to do.

It asks me what you're doin' when I don't find you at home

And it tells me what to do to you when I get you alone."

The flames danced around the singer's head as his voice rose.

"I got the fire in my head, still be burning when I'm dead blues..."

"I do know you," Holyoak said softly. The playing stopped and the figure looked at him, little tongues of fire dancing like a twinkle in his eye. "Fire in My Head Blues," Holyoak said, half a smile cracking his lips. You're Ledhead Johnston."

"At your service, sir. I'm glad you know my song." Ledhead began to play again. It was old now, but everybody knew that song. Only it was supposed to be fast and rolling, but the way he played now was slow and sad as a dirge, and that sweet, soft voice like old leather was full of murder.

"There's a fire in my head, girl, and you know it's burning hot,

That Ol' Masser the Devil put it to remind me what he's bought.

It can't be soothed, not even by the cold wind through the pines,

And it burns bright behind my eyes even in the deepest mines.

"I got the fire in my head, still be burning when I'm dead blues..."

"So it's true then, isn't it?" Holyoak asked. "The Devil buying your soul for guitar lessons, filling your head with burning pain that only got worse until you lost your mind?" Sparks flew from Ledhead's brow as he cocked an eyebrow, but he kept playing and singing, his voice becoming like a low growl.

"Oh that fire in my head, girl, it sure is burning me,
But it pays the water and the gas and the electricity.
It makes the gee-tar sing, and gives the fingertips a thrill,
And when I'm dead and gone that fire will be burning still.

"I got the fire in my headbone, still be burning when I'm dead 'n' gone—"

"That's it," Holyoak interrupted. The tempo and the force with which the strings where plucked had been building but the playing again abruptly stopped.

"What's what?" Ledhead asked, the menace that had been responsible for the massacre in this house manifesting itself in his voice.

"Dead and gone," Holyoak said flatly. "They found your head in the railway tracks, but they never found your body. That was almost 20 years ago."

"This my body right here," Ledhead said defiantly.

"It might be," Holyoak said thoughtfully, trying to inch his hand toward the shells in his belt. "Let's find out."

Suddenly, Ledhead loomed over him, stretching his body unnaturally and exposing the twisted muscle and tendons of his neck and chest over the guitar. With one motion, Holyoak slid two fingers and his thumb over a pair of shells in his belt, dropped them in the break, snapped it closed and fired twice. Ledhead spat and coughed as he sank back into his seat, great gobs of gore and coagulated blood falling over the guitar and a pattern of rotten flesh splayed across the wall behind him. He screamed primally as the smoke cleared.

Holyoak's body was still rigid. The Lord was usually in his movements when he struck down the wicked, but though his hands and his eyes had proven true, he had not felt Him.

"It's not enough my woman got to leave me!" Ledhead bellowed. "It's not enough I got to be a slave that can never be free! GOD HISSELF got to send some holy hitman to keep me down!" He rose again from the chair, brandishing the guitar over his head and rushing towards Holyoak, who slipped backwards on some piece of one of the Clays and fell as he tried to step away. Ledhead's heavy steps reverberated into his head through the floorboards as he came to stand over him with the guitar held high.

"Oh my God," a woman's voice said from the doorway. Holyoak managed to crane his neck around wildly and saw Mabel standing there. "What is he?" she asked, even her deep fear unable to keep the southern syrup out of her voice. "He's no ghost so what is he?"

"Mabel!" he spat. "Get out of here!"

Holyoak swallowed the panic like bile at the back of his throat, searching for the Lord in his heart. At last he felt the familiar glow. It started in his chest but didn't move into his hands as it usually did. He opened his mouth, and "Sounds like a song to me," came out. He had no explanation for where that thought had come from except that it came from God.

Ledhead shuffled his feet, trying the weight of the instrument in his hands. "Yeah," he said, a look of confusion forming and then clearing on his molten-lead face. "Yeah... it does at that." He smiled, lowering the guitar in his hands and plucking the strings, randomly at first, a song forming more quickly than before.

"*Oh my woman left me in the long night all alone,*
Left me in that black country with no place to call my own."

Holyoak squinted as Ledhead began to fade around the edges, blur and disappear. His voice still carried, sounding further and further away.

"I ain't got time to cry about it or put it in a song,
But everybody to the top they tryin' to do me wrong."

Flames spilled out from where he had stood, surrounding Holyoak. Mabel grabbed him under the arms and dragged him halfway to his feet and out the door. He finally found his footing in the dirt outside, taking her roughly by the arm and pulling her into the dark where he had left the truck. "I thought I said 2 o'clock!" he shouted between jagged breaths.

"Good thing I got here at 1," she said defiantly as she struggled to keep up in her heels.

"I got those no soul left and no money,
And now God put a hit on me blues."

They dove behind the truck, only to have shards of glass thrown over them as the flames shattered all the windows and tore the top of the vehicle clean off.

"I think you nearly did yourself in," Mabel said, laying a salved bandage across his arm and letting her hand lie there just a little too long.

Holyoak shifted in his seat on her porch and rifled impatiently through his dogeared little book of psalms. His lip twitched nervously, so slightly that it would have gone unnoticed had it not tipped the cigarette in the corner of his mouth up and down.

"Well now Mr. Reverend," she said, hands on her hips, her voice smoky and sweet—especially with that edge of anger in it. "There's a time for prayer books and a time for looking at the world. Why," she continued, waving her arm towards her yard, "you ain't even mentioned that shiny new car there by the house."

He raised an eyebrow at it, shiny black in the sun like a magnificent bug, and took the creaky wooden stairs down from the porch to look at it.

"What is it?" he asked.

"It's the Clays' car. A brand new '57 Chevrolet Bel Air," she began loudly before lowering her voice out of respect. "Mayor figures that since they don't need it anymore and since you lost your truck doing this town such a good turn that it should be yours. The Clays got no kin, so he had the papers made up this morning."

"What about the boy?" he asked.

"We take care of our own in Tennessee if that's what you're asking," she said pressing her eyebrows together. "But he ain't old enough to drive."

"Perfect for my quiet drives in the country," he mocked, but he smiled to himself as he looked over the smooth lines of the car.

"Well!" she exclaimed, and he watched over his shoulder as she turned quickly back to the house with a twirl of her pale red hair. "And here I was thinking I might do you a good turn this morning too, unless your King David has something to say about it." The door slammed shut and he looked heavenward.

"No," he said softly, flicking the cigarette out into the yard as he turned and went up to the house. "David was a sinner too."

He left town alone in the night in that shiny new automobile. He decided to try its radio and turned the dial only to find himself confronted again by that faux-creepy voice between the static:

"Hello, boys and ghouls, your pal, the Kustom Kreeper, has a real treat for you tonight!" Holyoak reached for the dial in disgust and was just about to turn it off when the voice continued: "Yes just for you, it's a brand new Ledhead Johnston song! Wonder where they dug this up? Hee hee. This is coming to us as a special preview from Studd Records, home of 'That Three-Nail Sound' and it's going out to some loyal listener named Holyoak—what a name friends!—from the Old Master up there, saying 'Thanks for the inspiration, I'll be keeping an eye on you.' Well, boos and bats but that doesn't sound *kreepy* at all, hee hee."

Holyoak clenched his jaw as the music started and pressed his foot a little harder on the gas as he moved down the blacktop into the dark.

"*Oh I'm living like a slave that can't ever be free,*
I'm working for my Ol' Masser in those fields of eternity.

"*I ain't got a dime or a diamond mine to buy my way to peace*
'Cause all the dollars that I had I couldn't take with me.

"*I got those no soul left and no money,*
And now God put a hit on me blues."

And it was fast, and loud, and rolling, like all Ledhead's best songs were.

Ghost Town

THE REV. Holyoak had found himself in Arizona again, chasing down another lost soul. Christine Whitt's daddy was convinced that it was more than her just running away. He was sure it had something to do with a local legend about a string of ghost towns full of dead men. Actually, Holyoak would have used the word obsessed. He wasn't sure how Whitt had found him, or where he'd connected his daughter to the gruesome legend, but he didn't ask those kind of questions. He went where the Lord led him.

So far, none of his leads had panned out, but his digging had put him into contact with the Silver Sabremen Lodge in Prescott. He had found this men's club to be mostly a bunch of meddlesome kooks, but their fascination with the obscure and occult, initially seeming to be only that typical of fraternal organizations of bored middle-class men, only disturbed him more when found to be not only genuine but exceptionally well-studied. Fortunately, they were generous with their knowledge and had been allowing him supervised access to their library.

Today his watcher was a graying, subtly widening Greg Hilsson. Holyoak had been given to understand that Hilsson was something of an important figure in the Sabremen, himself visiting from back East. Looking at him in his plain suit and rhinestone decorated fez, he sensed that he certainly felt himself to be important and couldn't help but wonder why he'd volunteered to watch him.

"I think you'll find this volume has a more precise telling of the legend," Hilsson said, placing a heavy volume on the desk next to him. Holyoak nodded curtly and kept reading. Hilsson sat back down and watched him, and after a moment, Holyoak took a look at the offered tome.

"Thank you," he said gruffly.

"You know," Hilsson said, crossing his palms in his lap and letting his head roll to one side. "We've heard of you, Reverend."

"And?" he asked, lifting his gaze from the page.

"Well," Hilsson continued, sucking air between his teeth. He had a broad, midwestern way of speaking that made Holyoak impatient. "A mysterious town, in league with the Devil, halfway into death, raiding the world of the living… This legend you're investigating—just why has it called your attention."

Holyoak let the book lie on the table. "A girl went missing. Her father seems to think this 'legend' has something to do with it."

"And what, Reverend, do you think?"

"I've seen enough in my days—especially in this desert."

"We know." Hilsson sat back, satisfied.

"Where did you lot find this book?" Holyoak asked. He had expected another conflicting, vague account, but this book had an entire chapter about a cluster of failed towns about a hundred miles west that had been believed wiped out by plague in the 1850s but from which mysterious raids appeared to originate for decades after. It went on to detail how someone named "Brother Tull" had wiped them out, finding them corrupted by supernatural evil.

"There are maybe a couple of dozen copies of that book in the world. It's not a book you'll find outside of one of our Lodges. The Tull that this book speaks of was the founder of this Lodge that you're sitting in now—one of our heroes, especially for our brothers in Arizona."

"But if this Tull wiped them all out—"

"Tull himself suspected that there was one town that he couldn't find: a place called Delilah. But he never picked up that there was a pattern." Hilsson pulled a piece of tracing paper from his pocket and pulled the book towards him. Holyoak craned his neck to see him place it over the map in the book. Drawn on the translucent paper was a complicated sigil. "This is the sign of Pestilentia," he said. Laid over the map its points lined up exactly with the locations of the extinct towns. "And this," Hilsson said, pointing to a place which was empty on the map but indicated by a long limb of the bizarre symbol, "this is Delilah."

"Do you think it's really still there?" Holyoak asked, knowing the answer.

Hilsson nodded slowly. "We do. We were aware of the Whitt girl going missing, and she hasn't been the only one. We're going to investigate now that we have some idea where to look. In fact, it's fallen to me to decide if you should join us."

"I drive."

Hilsson pretended to be taken aback. "I didn't say you were."

Holyoak smiled, fastening the top buttons of his shirt and replacing his white collar. "Yes, you did."

Holyoak approached the town again slowly. It was rough and unused roads that took them there—roads that weren't on any map and barely qualified as roads. It had taken hours to navigate the treacherous country. His throat was dry and he felt a great sympathy for the black paint job of his Bel Air, covered in dust. He closed his eyes and whispered in God's ear for a moment as the sparse main street of Delilah rose into view, like something lost in time.

"What was that?" Hilsson asked from the passenger seat. There were two of his fezzed lodge brothers in the back seat, and they pushed themselves forward to look at the weathered old town.

"Just a prayer," Holyoak said, his jaw clenching as he stopped the car. There were townsfolk milling around slowly.

"Good. George, did you prepare the wards?"

"Finishing them now," one of the men in the back seat said, and Holyoak heard him whispering something, chantlike and low.

"Is that a prayer?" Holyoak asked.

"No," Hilsson replied, with something like patience.

The four men exited the car and moved down the center of the street. Being closer to the townspeople, they saw that they did appear diseased. Their skin was shriveled and gray, and they moved as if insensible of their surroundings. Their clothes were old fashioned, and the colors had faded to dingy grays. A woman and her child, a little girl, almost walked into Holyoak crossing the street.

"Beggin' your pardon, sir," the woman said, averting her eyes, and he saw that much of one side of her face, hidden though it was by her bonnet, appeared to have rotted away.

A man in preacher's black stood in the street, his milky eyes unseeing as they approached.

"Welcome, strangers," he said. His preacher's collar was red and curious hooking designs were embroidered into the lapels of his coat in the same color. "Have you come to worship the Lord?"

"We each worship in our way," Hilsson responded.

"The services begin soon," the preacher said. "Come join our sabbath meal. Worship the Lord who sustains us and gives us life and strength."

The strange figure looked as if he had little of either, so Holyoak asked. "And which Lord is that?"

"Why," the old man seemed puzzled, "the True Lord, and him only."

"Of course, brother," Hilsson said, before Holyoak could respond. "We go to him now." The frail figure turned, and they followed him towards the church at the other end of town. Pale figures with cold eyes observed them as they moved closer, and Holyoak, his senses alert, noticed a thin man in a black hat who seemed to pay them special attention, stopping to watch them as they passed.

The church itself was much like you'd find in any small town that was old enough. The whole town in fact looked like something out of a western movie set that had been allowed to sit and rot. The church was the best kept building in the town, but the top of its steeple had broken off and lay, its cross bent, in the dirt. The paint on the church was horribly chipped and dusty but had clearly been a deep black.

They entered the church and found it modestly decorated, but it was a black cloth with an inverted red star stitched in that draped the pulpit.

There was a muffled cry as two haggard beings dragged in a girl who was roughly tied and gagged. They were dressed in the same outdated style as the rest of the people he had seen, and their skin seemed especially gray with their claw-like hands against the rosy, living flesh of the girl.

In an instant, Holyoak lashed out, both of his great fists swinging, and a brittle breaking sounded when he made contact with the skulls of the girl's captors. Hilsson grabbed her and quickly drew her into a circle formed by him and the other Sabremen, whose hands shot up in an arcane gesture as the almost skeletal figures tried to right themselves. "Christine Whitt?" he asked, and the girl shrieked through the dirty cloth in her mouth in response. Holyoak swung aside his thick bomber jacket, quickly leveling a sawed-off shotgun at his hip and blasting them apart.

A long whistle sounded from the door.

"Reeves!" the old preacher shouted, staring blindly in the direction of the sound. Holyoak and his party turned and saw a particularly ugly example of the type they'd been seeing in this town. "These unbelievers have taken the sacrifice."

"Our Lord ain't gonna like that," said Reeves, letting his words sit in the air. He pushed back the brim of his black hat and stared at Holyoak with cold gray eyes. His face was so mottled and pale that Holyoak was at last certain that the people of this town were not alive in any godly sense. A scruffy beard framed his face and filled the deep hollows of his cheeks, and a chip of bone protruded from the flattened hole where his nose should have been. "Nope. Our Lord ain't gonna like that a bit. Good thing Jarvis spotted them tramping through town."

He walked up to Holyoak and pointed at his collar. "You're a preacher man. You understand that sacrifices got to be made for religion. The Lord keeps us livin', but somebody else has got to pay him back."

"Tell me about your lord." Holyoak was unmoving. Reeves was dry as a husk, but there was a charnel stench on his breath.

"I told you!" the preacher interrupted. He seemed baffled by their ignorance. "We serve and worship the True Lord of the Earth and Under-the-Earth. The Lord Satan."

"Now we're getting somewhere." Holyoak said, leveling his shotgun at Reeves.

"Oh, holy man," he mocked. "Where was your God when this town was poor and hungry and dying from the sickness? Where was the Lord of Heaven when the babies sucked at their mama's cold titties and the hounds picked at the bones of their masters? So our new god likes a little nip of blood now and then, and likes to watch us raise a little hell. We here all these years, and we ain't going on account of you."

"It was when the pox came that we called him," the preacher interjected. "Oh, we called him and he came. He cleansed the valley with fire and kept us all here, undying, forever. Praise him! All hail!"

"All hail," Reeves responded by rote.

Holyoak was full of righteous anger and moved the shortened barrel closer to his foe. Reeves raised his hands, but exposed a brown, toothy smile, pointing with his chin at the bodies of his men lying on the floor. At first Holyoak thought that he was seeing bugs crawl towards the corpses. It was Hilsson who shouted: "The bodies, they're reforming! Take the girl, now!" he commanded his men, and they bolted for the door with her between them. Reeves began a laugh that sounded human at first until a deep, rasping rattle entered in from somewhere in his guts.

The door of the church burst open and more of Reeves' men entered, guns drawn. In an instant the Sabremen were down and the girl was running back into the church. Holyoak grabbed her and rolled back into the pews, the shotgun spewing the hot lead death of the second charge. Hilsson, with a speed that surprised him, dove behind the pulpit and the hoary preacher collapsed, riddled with holes, as Reeves and his men launched an indiscriminate spray of bullets in his direction.

Holyoak shouted over the den as he reloaded. "Your father sent me. I'll get you out of this"—a bullet struck the pew by his ear—"I'm not sure how, but God will show us." Holyoak heard Hilsson's voice rising from behind the pulpit. Suddenly he stood up, shouting a word or a phrase in some dead language. Holyoak again felt a bullet fly past his head, but realized it was the same one, shooting back out of the wood. Reeves and his men fell in a pile by the door and Holyoak realized in the sudden silence that all their bullets had been turned back on them.

"How did you do that?" he asked as they emerged from their cover.

"It doesn't matter," Hilsson said. "It won't last. The spells keeping them alive are too strong. We have to go."

The girl cried out when Holyoak pulled out his bowie knife, but calmed when he cut her ropes and even smiled weakly when he removed the gag. Hilsson had already checked to find his lodge brothers dead and was heading out into the street. The girl stopped above the remains of Reeves, which sat up against the wall. She was shouting and stomping on his body, but then froze in a terror so stiff that Holyoak had to forcibly pull her away.

Hilsson was squinting in the sun as he moved towards the Bel Air, and Holyoak had to support the girl as he followed. The people of the town had come out and stood along both sides of the street, watching them with sad, dead eyes. The same woman and little girl that had almost walked into him were there and he saw the child's eyes—still innocent but so very old.

The Whitt girl remained still as they got into the Bel Air and drove away back to the main road. They hadn't seen that Reeves had moved when she kicked him. It was only one eye that did, but it looked right at her. She felt as if he had seen her soul.

Holyoak sat alone in the library while Hilsson held an emergency meeting with the other members of the Lodge, reflecting on everything that he had seen. Men had died and it hadn't phased him the way it once did.

Hilsson entered. "A Sabreman seeks knowledge, Reverend," he said, as if reading his thoughts. "Our brothers are resting in that knowledge now."

"Doesn't your brotherhood believe in God?" he asked.

"It is part of every Sabreman's oath that he confess the One God—all others are false, or are his aspects."

Holyoak's eyes smoldered while he considered his words. "But that looked like some kind of witchery you used back there. Can you use the same weapons as God's enemies to do his work?"

Hilsson gestured towards Holyoak's shotgun that lie on the table like a sleeping animal. "Is a gun good or evil?"

"Man is good or evil. The gun is only an instrument."

Hilsson was silent a moment. "We are not sorcerers, Reverend. We are scientists. Keepers and practitioners of primeval knowledge. We're using that in what we believe is God's work."

Holyoak looked distant. "I know God has a mission for me. I don't yet know what it is—not the big picture of it. But he's guided my hand many times, brought me into the path of the unrighteous," he held up his hands, more the gnarled hands of a prizefighter than those of a holy man. "And through me he has struck them down." Holyoak sighed deeply. "I have prayed for him to show me what he asks of me, so that my soul can find some kind of peace."

Now it was Hilsson who considered his words. "Then we aren't so very different." Hilsson smiled. "We just don't believe in prayer."

Holyoak smiled back, indicating the shelves of esoteric books, the trays of fine liquor, and the erotic art that lined the room. "No, this doesn't look like a church."

"I'd like to show you something." Hilsson rose, producing a large ring of keys as he led him to the back of the library. "Only those with the rank of Adept can enter this room, and only those of my rank,"—he pointed to the word "Mage" emblazoned on his fez—"can admit a nonmember." There was a heavy door of iron bars there with the words "LIBRIS PROHIBITIS" above it. He opened it with a very old key.

There was a heavy feeling in the room. Looking around, Holyoak saw rows of ancient, leather-bound books gilt with indecipherable devices and a hideous statue that seemed to move when he looked at it in the corner of his eye. The rest of the art in the room was blatantly obscene.

Hilsson smiled boyishly and indicated a reinforced glass cabinet at the very back.

Holyoak drew closer as he used a separate key to open it, revealing a myriad of bottles, vials, and jars, thick with dust, and a crossed pair of Colt 45s which were conspicuously shining and clean. "Is this where you keep the bat's wings and eye of newt?" he asked.

"No," Hilsson beamed. "Those reagents are not forbidden. We keep those upstairs. These"—Hilsson said indicating the guns, "are the holy guns of Abramelin Tull, who used them to lay the walking dead in the frontier days of this state."

Holyoak felt a strange fascination for the guns. The weapons he had used up until now in his quest seemed crude. "May I?" he asked, his hands already reaching for them. Hilsson nodded and he took them up. The grips were carved with curious patterns of spirals and symbols that he had never seen before. They felt as if they had been made for his hands, but they made him uneasy.

Hilsson had a satisfied expression. "As I said, we don't believe in prayer. These are the only weapons that can break the dark magic being used to keep that town alive and in league with the darkness."

"Then why didn't we take them with us?" Holyoak asked.

"Reverend, Tull left those weapons there in that spot himself. He made this territory safe, built this lodge, and hung those guns there. He said God was done with them and done with him and he died. No brother has been able to lift those guns from that spot for 75 years, as if they didn't want to be taken."

"That's easy to say when I've already done it," Holyoak said skeptically.

"Maybe." Hilsson looked at him gravely. "But I know all the brothers here tried when they heard about the trouble starting again. Hell, I flew all the way from Indiana to try it myself. Our mistake was pride, thinking it could only be one of us. Don't ask me to explain, but when I saw you fighting Reeves' men in Delilah I could tell: Those guns were waiting for you."

Holyoak couldn't sleep that night. Two men had been killed quickly in front of him. Killed by monsters of hell. This should have been his mission alone. He became aware of an icy presence and looked up to see the girl watching over him in the dark.

"What are you doing, Christine?" he asked.

"I have to go back," she said, her voice toneless except for a tinge of fear.

"You should stay with me," he said. "I won't let anything happen to you."

She hesitated, but slid into the bed beside him. He shifted, positioning himself over her and pulling her hands up to the headboard. She practically purred, pushing her hips against his and letting her eyes roll as she arched her back. Too late she found her hands tied to the bedpost. Holyoak sat up abruptly. "Sorry, Christine," he said. He stood up and moved to the door, taking the holstered guns of Abramelin Tull from the coat rack where he had hung them. "I can smell Reeves' magic on you."

Christine protested, the frosty glare of foreign influence glinting in her eyes, and she watched him as he considered placing the gun belts on his hips, only to wrap them over his shoulder.

"Too much power for you, holy man!" she spat in a voice not her own. And they did in fact pulse with an uneasy and otherworldly charge. Christine's face changed. "Help me!" she cried. "Don't let them take me back!" She shrieked and now she was pleading, confused as her own will struggled against Reeves' unnatural pull. "You must let me go, Reeves and his Lord call me!"

"But my Lord calls him to account. And their sorrows shall be multiplied that hasten after another God."

The air above the dirt road that cut through Delilah wavered in the heat of the noon sun. Holyoak wiped the sweat from his brow as he squinted over the dashboard, the wheels of the Bel Air growling over the dry, soft clay. He felt for the Colt 45s that lay in their holsters on the seat beside him coiled like snakes and drew them closer. He parked the car across from the dilapidated saloon. Reeves and his fellows stood waiting for him across the way, with black hats and with spurs on their boots, their gray-mottled skin almost blindingly pale in the harsh light. A few similarly deformed faces watched from the windows of the establishment as Holyoak opened the door and placed his own boots in the dust.

He was a broad, heavily built man, and wouldn't have looked as tall as he was if he wasn't standing by the car as he put the old but well cared for gun belts around his waist. Reeves' pale lips widened into a snarling smile as he and his men stepped forward, three on each side of him, their white, bony fingers hovering over the grips of the pistols at their sides. "You ready to try your Lord against mine?" Reeves asked, and spit a pus-filled wad of tobacco juice towards him.

"Always."

"Good," Reeves said.

As if on cue, he and his men all drew. Before they got off a shot, three lay in the dirt, black blood oozing slowly from their faces. Holyoak couldn't deny that the guns felt right in his hands. Holyoak was fast, but not faster than all of them together. Two more shots rang out, missing him, but Reeves' was as fast as he was and had already put two bullets into Holyoak, in his left shoulder and arm. Only now did the pain register, a thrilling shock of cold through his body coming on after the warm wetness inside his sleeve. "Blessed be the Lord my strength, who teacheth my hands to war, and my fingers to fight." He staggered forward. He could only hold onto the Colt in his left hand loosely, a mere symbol of power. But with the right he fired twice more, and two more fell, but not before one got off a shot that hit him in the right side of the chest and made him gasp for air. "My goodness, and my fortress," he continued, forcing his steps to be surer. A crack came from Reeves gun and Holyoak felt his right leg give out. He looked down at the slick red staining his jeans and realized Reeves was playing with him. He looked up and saw him and his last remaining man watching him with a cold glee in their hard eyes. "My high tower, and my deliverer. My shield." Holyoak swayed on his feet, and Reeves' man made the mistake of aiming coyly at his head. Holyoak fired again, successfully hitting his would-be killer between the eyes before collapsing in the street.

Reeves' spurs jangled as he walked to his prone body. Holyoak looked up, the taste of bloody mud caking his mouth. "You poor bastard," Reeves conceded, leaning over him, the smell of decay and rancid black chaw heavy in his face. "You've seen the magic. My boys'll be right as rain before the sun sets, but what about you?"

Holyoak grinned, his mouth full of blood.

"What you grinnin' at, boy?"

Holyoak struggled, his voice raspy and tight. "Look closer," he managed to say nodding his head at the gun in his right hand. Reeves face fell when he saw the signs of power carved in the grip around the name TULL. He looked at his men and saw no magic moving to restore them. He tried to back away.

"Cast forth lightning, and scatter them," Holyoak said hoarsely and shot him in the kneecap, which flew off bloodlessly in a cloud of dust. "Shoot out thine arrows, and destroy them!" Reeves stepped backwards painfully, causing the damaged limb to crack off at the knee. He fell backwards, his gun rolling away in the dirt. Holyoak dragged himself through the dusty road, past Reeves' severed shin, still standing in its boot. Reeves was whimpering softly, reaching desperately for his gun as Holyoak dragged himself up over his desiccated body.

"Satan! Help me!" Reeves screamed with a dry rattle in his throat. Holyoak thought he looked utterly pitiful, like something that you'd scrape off the bottom of your boot.

"Not as much fun when it's a fair fight, is it?" Holyoak asked. He propped himself up with his bleeding arm as best he could, and with his other hand shaking, pointed a Colt in Reeves' face. "Give my regards to your lord." The sound of the bullet split the air, accompanied by a hollow thud as the back of Reeves' head scattered, painting the dull tan of the unpaved street sticky black and gray.

Holyoak awoke suddenly. The pain reminded him quickly of all the places he'd been shot, but it was the hard wood of the table at his back that had awakened him. Christine was above him, pressing down with a blood-red cloth at the wound in his chest. He could see she'd been crying but her face was concentrated and resolute—and her own. She only stared at him.

"Ah," Hilsson said, stepping into view above him. "You're awake."

"What happened?" he asked.

"Christine managed to fight off Reeves' influence long enough to tell us that you had set off here on your own. By the time we got here you'd already taken care of him and his men." Hilsson adjusted a bandage on his arm and Holyoak noticed that it had some strange script written on it. "Oh, just a little healing spell to hold you over 'til the hospital, nothing to worry about." Holyoak tried to protest but didn't have the strength and he relaxed against the rough grain of his makeshift sick bed. "That was a foolish thing to do, coming here alone."

"Maybe," Holyoak whispered, "but it was the right thing to do."

"Look!" Christine interjected. Both her hands were still pressed against his chest, but he followed her stare out the window. A crowd of townspeople was moving away slowly into the desert. He saw their preacher, his head low and shoulders slumped, walking alone, apart from the others. The little girl he'd seen before turned back and raised a hand towards him slowly before her mother took her and led her away.

"They're tired," Hilsson said sadly. "Only Reeves and his men wanted this to keep going. The rest have known for a long time that they got a bum deal and they want to rest. Thankfully, it was easy for us to release them from the spell once Reeves' magic was broken." Hilsson looked mournfully after them. "All this so that they could go on living a half a life and keep their town going in this godforsaken desert."

"They have called the people happy, that hath these things: but happy is that people whose God is the Lord."

Hilsson smiled. "I've spoken to my counterpart at the Prescott lodge and he agrees. Sacred arms like those guns choose their own partners. The brotherhood will be entrusting them with you."

"I can't—" he began, but he knew that he would.

"It's already done, and you are counted among the friends of the Lodge," Hilsson said, pushing Holyoak's tensing body back to the table. "You said God has a mission for you and we know he has a purpose for those guns. For now at least, you ride together."

Drive-Out

HOLYOAK MOVED carefully, painfully aware of the lithe young girl who was following just too close for her safety. He wanted her near—for practical reasons. He needed to be able to keep eyes on her if the specter appeared suddenly. It didn't have anything to do with her graceful little feet in those little black flats, her curly, golden ponytail, or the way she made that bullet bra look like she was born with it. No, he had to be able to see her, at least peripherally. Red Jack had claimed too many girls just like her.

The drive-in was packed, despite the murders that had happened here around this time for the past few years. Space and privacy were at a premium for teenagers, and they had been willing to overcome the fear. Mabel, the girl who was very nearly stepping on his feet, had come running to him for help. A few kids had been spooked by the lone man in the black Bel Air, but even over his bomber jacket she had seen the starched white collar in his plain black shirt.

"I need your help, reverend!" she panted, running to the car. The window was already pulled down, and he feigned surprise at her sudden appearance, but he had seen her. He was watching everything, like a hawk on a telephone pole by a dusty, two-lane blacktop. He was aware of everything that was happening at this drive-in, even what passed for a plot in this badly dubbed Mexican wrestler movie. He had even counted the little specks in the image that seemed to be little stains on the projector lens.

"What can I do, miss?" he asked calmly.

"My friend, Lola," she was talking and breathing so fast, she could barely get the words out. "She went off with Tommy Watson, and she didn't come back."

"I don't know your friend, miss," Holyoak said in his best patient-preacher voice. "But—is that unusual for her?"

The girl blushed visibly, even in the dim and flickering light of the big projector. "She's not that kind of girl. She'd be back before anything…"

"That's okay, miss…"

"Lewis. Mabel Lewis."

"Miss Mabel Lewis. I only mean, what makes you so worried."

"I know they say they're only stories—about Red Jack I mean—but…"

"But you saw something?"

Mabel shook her head. She was starting to cry.

"They aren't only stories, Mabel." Holyoak's voice was low and grave. "Tell me what you saw."

"A figure, moving in the trees around the drive in. He was in the shadows, but he was lit up. Like he…"

"Like he was on fire, Mabel?"

She nodded vigorously. "Yes, you believe me, don't you?"

Holyoak did, and said so.

"It's just, Dale—that's Dale Mahone, my boyfriend—he's been making fun of me all night."

"And where is Dale now?"

Mabel looked embarrassed. "He saw it too. He ran away." She ventured: "Is it really him, Red Jack?"

Holyoak nodded. That was what they called him now. Jack Dunbar had been a pretty typical teenage delinquent until the town's new drive-in gave him a more or less private spot to rough up his girlfriends. It didn't take him long to realize he liked cutting them too, and soon girls' bodies started being found in the woods that circled the theater lot. When the police caught up with him, holed up in the projector booth, he hadn't gone quietly.

Since then, every year around this time, a girl or two had gone missing. The drive-in would close, the police would investigate, but the case would go unsolved, and the business at the drive-in would eventually return to normal. If a body was found, it was invariably out in the woods.

Wracked with guilt, the theater's owners had reached out to him, after trying a priest, a rabbi, and a moth-eaten private detective. Holyoak had already dug up Jack's bullet-ridden corpse in the town cemetery and salted and burned what remained. He had hoped that would be the end of it, but he had camped out the last few nights to check for any sign of further manifestation.

"Mabel," he said patiently as he crept to the woods now with her in tow, "I need you close, but I need a little more arm room than you're giving me." She looked both confused and flustered, more so when Holyoak reached into either side of his jacket and produced his guns.

He realized by the look on her face that she had probably never seen a gun up close—at least not more than an innocuous hunting rifle in her father's den. These were magnificent specimens: gigantic, silver-handled, antique Colt 45s weapons of death and slaughter, devices made to kill men and monsters.

There was orange light and the sounds of movement on the other side of a line of trees. There was a gurgling grunt, followed by a horrible, gagged scream. Holyoak put a finger over his lips and moved down through the cover. There he was, Red Jack in his tight leather jacket, bloodied switchblade in hand. His pompadour was a lick of flame that flared when he turned to the intruders. He smiled viciously, wiping the crimsoned knife on his jeans.

There was a teenage boy on the ground, clutching at the gory mess of his stomach. A teenage girl in a torn dress was tied up and gagged next to him.

"Lola!" Mabel shrieked, her arm up over her face, her body unsure of whether to run to her friend or just run away.

"Here for the show, preacher man?" the ghostly figure asked. His voice had a far away, static sound to it. Holyoak noticed that his skin didn't just glow like fire but flickered. There was a clue to this, but his brain was scrambling to connect the dots.

"When you get back to Hell," Holyoak growled through gritted teeth. "Tell your boss the Reverend Holyoak says hello."

If a ghost could go pale, then Red Jack did. Word was getting around in bad places. Holyoak noticed that they were on a small hill. He could see the drive-in screen from here, as well as the back of the projector booth.

"You don't scare me, preacher man" Red Jack tried to laugh. Holyoak raised his guns and fired simultaneously. The silver bullets passed through the ghost, leaving only a dark cloud in the air and the smell of smoke. But Red Jack reformed quickly in a flash of hot flame behind Lola. He pulled her to her feet, holding his knife to her throat. She screamed through the gag as his touched burned her arm. Holyoak noticed that where he touched her, he warped—like an image projected on a surface that isn't flat.

"Alright," Holyoak said, lowering his guns. His attention was on the projector booth in the corner of his eye. He spoke softly: "He hath bent his bow, and made it ready."

Red Jack smiled wryly. "Praying won't help her!" Lola whimpered as he pressed the point of his switchblade into her throat, producing a small trickle of blood.

"He hath also prepared for him the instruments of death." Holyoak's gaze was intense with righteous fire as he stared at the ghost. His voice was louder now. "He ordaineth his arrows against the persecutors!" Quick as lightning, Holyoak fired, not at Red Jack, but through the windows of the booth at the far-away projectors, which exploded in sparks. Red Jack flickered out, a surprised look on his face. A crackling scream split the air, immediately receding into great distance. Lola fell to the ground, Mable rushing to her and removing the gag and the ropes.

They were on the road again, now. Lola was in the back seat of the Bel Air, frantically pressing her boyfriend's varsity jacket against his bleeding guts. It was bad, but he'd make it.

Mabel was curled up in the seat right next to Holyoak as he drove them to the nearest hospital. "The police made such a mess of Jack when they shot him down in that projection booth," he explained. "There must have been a little blood on the lens or the bulbs. Just enough to keep Red Jack tethered to this world." He patted her back, assuring her that it was all over.

"I don't think I'll be going to the drive-in anymore," she said. "It hasn't been fun anyway since I finished high school."

Holyoak coughed. "Do you think Dale made it out okay?"

She snuggled closer to him, but they were safe now and her being close wasn't a problem. She sighed sleepily. "Who?"

Hell Camino

"MAYBE I'VE got what you need." The voice was cool and feminine. It startled him and he hit his head against the underside of the popped hood of his Bel Air. He hadn't seen a single car on this road for hours and he was sure he hadn't heard anybody pull up.

He turned around, irritable until he saw her standing there. She winked a dark Spanish eye at him winsomely. Her black, leather coveralls squeaked as she shifted her hips. She held out a large wrench in her perfectly manicured, long, red fingernailed hand.

Taking the wrench, Holyoak gulped, tugging at his open shirt neck. He knew he was a good-looking man. This kind of thing always happened when he took off his cleric's collar. He took a quick glance at the little band of starched white linen that was currently sitting in his passenger seat.

"Thank you, miss...?" he asked, trying not to notice the way that her perfect, tanned breasts pressed against her neckline. Her coveralls were not doing a good job living up to their name.

"Just call me..." she raised one of her perfectly arched eyebrows and looked around coyly with those big, dark eyes. "...Jezebel," she decided, nodding her head assertively without disturbing a single hair in her black bangs. The nod caused her pulchritudinous bosoms to wobble against the tight confines of her neckline, relaxing with a triumphant jiggle as they popped her top button and revealed that her skin tan went at least a few inches deeper than modesty usually allowed.

"Xavier Holyoak," he said, catching himself gulping again. A twinge of guilt caused him to clarify: "Rev. Xavier Holyoak."

"Oh!" she exclaimed coquettishly, looking down at her neckline. "I'm sorry, Reverend. But you have to admit, it is hot out here. Reminds me of home."

No time to be distracted, Holyoak reminded himself. The people of Prescott, Arizona, were in trouble. Something evil was besieging their town and they needed professional help. That was why they had called him. He'd just managed to put down the sinister ghost that had been harassing some showgirls in Reno. Besides accepting a bit too much scotch, he had managed to avoid temptation in a city of sin. But he had a long way to go across this bleak desert and no time to waste.

"Thanks for the wrench," he said, turning back to his work under the hood. It was no use. The radiator was cracked. He needed to look busy. There was something wild and unnatural about this girl. She stepped up close behind him, her nails brushing his shoulder. She laid a hand there. Her breath was hot on the back of his neck as she peered over, ostensibly to examine his work.

"Of course, you could always hitch a ride with me," she said, pivoting around to rest her hips against his headlights. She nodded towards her own car.

He'd been so struck by the sight of her, that he hadn't seen it. A Chevy El Camino. Cherry red and jet black and perfect in every detail. Just as its driver. It glinted in the harsh Nevada sun.

If somebody was trying to keep him from getting to Prescott, they were pulling out all the stops.

Jezebel's hips swayed as she moved towards her car. Her tight, leather coveralls did next to nothing to hide her supple spine, quivering posterior, taught hamstrings or perfectly tapered calves. None of this caught Holyoak's attention more than the odd shape of her feet covered in knee-high, high-heeled boots.

"I see you noticed my feet," she smiled, her hand touching the shiny chrome passenger door handle. "It's just a... family trait."

She opened the door and sat down on the red leather seat. With her feet still on the ground, Holyoak got a better look at them. Was it hooves they reminded him of? She leaned forward, and his mind temporarily emptied of all such concerns as her neckline plunged and her coveralls again struggled to maintain whatever passed for her decency.

"After all, you'll never make it to Prescott with that clunker of yours."

Holyoak snapped out of it, staring her wild-eyed in the face. "How do you know about Prescott?" he demanded.

"Oh," she said with a dismissive wave of her hand. "I'm sure you mentioned it."

Before he could protest, Jezebel pulled her feet into the car, draping herself across the deep bucket seat.

"Anyway, better you get there at all, even if you have to take a little detour. My car is funny you see. It only goes South." She wrinkled her nose and laughed. Her laughter so sweet it sent chills up his spine.

She shifted in the seat, arching her back as her fingers gently caressed the chrome ball of the stick shift.

"I'll even let you drive."

Holyoak's eyes went up and down the curves of her body as he reminded himself that he was a man of God. Then his eyes moved along the curves of the El Camino and he let out a deep breath.

After all, a man of God is still a man.

"Alright," he said. "Maybe just to the next service station."

Goddess of Murder

I

THE LODGE was lit dimly as Holyoak entered, no light at all in fact, except from candles in brown glass on the tables spread around the room. The entrance to this lodge was set back, so that he wouldn't have a full view of the room until he took a few steps forward. A weird, throaty warble filled the air, and a jangle of many small bells, each delicate note piling on the others until it was a wall of clattering noise.

He pulled the great 45s from beneath his bomber jacket. Cautiously he stepped forward. The room had been rearranged to place a large dais at the far end, and upon it was a hideously feminine shape in some unfamiliar blue metal or stone. Its four slender arms and lithe legs seemed to move almost imperceptibly, but he realized after squinting at it that it was more like the air around it was shimmering. A long length of delicate silver chain lay coiled lazily on the floor around it.

The Sabremen were scattered in the space before the idol. Their eyes were red, hair unkempt, faces haggard. They moved in a jerking, wild dance, with spinning movements that had torn the sleeves loose from their suits. Ceremonial fezzes were askew or—unheard of within a Sabreman Lodge, discarded and trampled on the floor. Some held tambourines, others were wreathed in bells. One of their number saw Holyoak enter and shouted, hoarse-

MAC

voiced and wild-eyed. The others spun faster, ululating wildly.

There was a sudden rush of air as doors and windows were slammed open. Wild, hunched-over figures spilled in from every possible entrance into the lodge itself. They snarled and hissed, painted and manicured nails reaching towards him like the talons of some murderous birds. But despite their bestial movements, they were garbed in the best dresses and costume jewelry that he imagined their local department store had been able to provide, and while it was slipping from its intended arrangements, their hair was well-coifed in beauty parlor dos.

Holyoak searched for some opening in the drawing crowd that would get him to a door. Again, some Sabreman moaned plaintively. Hesitating, he put the guns away. Whatever happened, he couldn't use them against what he knew to be the Sabremen's wives, in whatever state they were in.

Glittering knives were being brandished by the changed women all around him now. He ducked one blow, instinctively trying to stop another with his left hand only to draw it back, stung and bloody. He raised his shoulders and balling his back, pushed his way through the crowd towards the open back door, feeling at least one or two blades turn powerlessly against the grain of his leather coat, clutching hands at his collar and his hair.

He rolled through the doorway and into the back yard, landing on his feet and leaping onto a patio table to get over the lodge fence. He hit the gravel on the other side unevenly, cursing foully as the pebbles embedded themselves into the leaking cut in his palm.

"Sorry, Lord," he whispered, looking skyward in the dark. He'd cut out across the side of the lodge house and could see several of the harpies prowling the lawn, knives drawn and teeth gnashing. He ran, softly on his boots, into the dark and back towards the town.

Holyoak closed the door carefully as he entered the house where he'd been staying. This was the house of Mrs. Clark—the widow Clark. He didn't want to think of her as Joanne, and yet he did. She was a young woman, very beautiful, bereft of a successful and attentive husband too soon.

He realized that silently as he had entered, he had disturbed her. She came from the kitchen in a modest but feminine chiffon nightgown. Her face and hair were immaculate, except for the pink puffiness around her eyes. She was drinking from a coffee cup and he could smell from where he stood that its contents weren't as innocent as her outfit.

"Rev. Holyoak," she acknowledged. They had each silently agreed to keep the emotional distance of titles and last names.

"Mrs. Clark," he responded, with a nod of his head.

"Can I make you a Sanka?" she asked.

"No," he said, "but you can make me a strong coffee." For the first time, he realized how wound up he was from his escape, and frankly how shaken. He rubbed the back of his hand against his perspiring brow.

"Are you alright?" Joanne—Mrs. Clark asked, setting her cup down on the coffee table and moving towards him. "You're trembling."

"I'm fine," he insisted, "but put some of whatever you put in yours in mine."

After a while the steadiness returned to his limbs as they sat silently in the living room.

"What did you find out?" she asked him at last.

"Well, your husband wasn't crazy." Holyoak knew that, but she didn't. Sabremen don't usually talk about the supernatural with their wives—are sworn not to, fact. But Ted had told Joanne things—bad things that had been happening at the lodge since a curious female idol of unknown origin had come into their possession.

"That's…" she hung her head "good to hear."

"Is it?" Holyoak asked, a little cruelly.

"I… don't know."

Holyoak softened his approach.

"Oh, of course it is, for his sake anyway. But it means that the things he told us were probably all true."

It had been Ted who had reached out to Holyoak for help. The first phone call had been merely concerned. Holyoak had been in Reno at the time, putting down a ghost that had been all too real, a relief after having handled one shortly before in Montana that had turned out to be a con.

The frauds were the easy jobs, and usually the ones where he actually got paid, but they left him cold and tired and disgusted with his fellow man. And they took him away from his important work, leaving the calling that God had placed on his conscience unsatisfied.

But the Sabremen were more expert than he was. If they were concerned about something it was probably authentic and dangerous. He'd headed southeast right away, checking in daily with Ted by phone. He'd had some car trouble and some woman trouble, and it had taken 5 days to get down to Prescott. He had met Ted briefly when he'd helped the Lodge out before, then as a regular contact in his work. He felt like he had gotten to know him over those calls—just enough anyway to be really worried when he seemed to be losing his grip. On his last call he seemed a man on the brink of madness from terror.

By the time Holyoak arrived he was dead.

"The idol is there, as weird as he described—or more so." He sighed. "He talked a lot about feeling its influence, and his lodge brothers seem to be completely gone."

"Why would he have…" She looked away. "…and not the others."

"I don't know—and there's something else. Have you heard from any of the wives?"

"I—I must have…" she said wringing her hands nervously. "My husband's just…" her eyes were welling up with tears.

"Hey," he said, taking her hands into his rough and calloused palms. "No time for that." He said it gently, but the urgency was there. "You've got to think, is there anything… different about the two of you?

She shrugged, shaking her head.

"It is strange," she said, almost to herself. "I haven't heard from the other wives. Oh, I'm not close to all of them, but Darla James, or Cindy Wright—her husband is Ted's—was Ted's—best friend."

Holyoak hesitated to tell her the rest of what he had seen. This situation was frightening enough without her friends and neighbors being turned into frothing-at-the-mouth, knife-toting lunatics.

"Damn!" Holyoak spat, punching his palm. "I'll have to go back. I need something to go on, but all the people that could tell me are dancing themselves to death in front of an obscene idol!"

"Tomorrow," Joanne said cautioning.

"You couldn't get me back there tonight!"

"I'll make up the couch for you," she said, rising to clear the dishes. Holyoak tried to help her and they fumbled a little too close. He could feel her breath and smell the natural sweetness of her hair and body. He was ashamed, but there he was. He was relieved when he saw something that brought him back to earth, hanging though it was down near the subtle cleavage between her smooth white breasts, just visible in that innocent nightgown.

"What's this?" he asked harshly, brushing the skin at her neck with his rough fingers as he touched the delicate, bizarrely formed necklace.

Also suddenly aware of herself, Joanne stepped back, clutching it. "It's just a necklace. A funny little man that lives outside the town made it. I always feel sorry for him when he comes into town with his wares, so I offered to buy it. But he gave it to me."

"We're going to see this 'funny little man.'"

"You mean this might have something to do with what's going on?"

Holyoak cocked an eyebrow and turned as if to go.

"Tomorrow," she said, pulling him back.

11

HOLYOAK SLEPT as well as could be expected in a cold living room on a hard couch with a beautiful woman a room away. That whole line of thinking was wrong on every level he could think of, but there it was—there she was—in the other room, which until recently she has shared with her husband. He shook the dim memory of an erotic dream out of his eyes as he rose up from the couch, his back and shoulders aching. He rolled his shoulders to get the kink out. No time for stiff muscles where his gun arms were concerned.

He had work to do.

Breakfast was prepared with technical skill. Eggs, bacon, toast and coffee, all in silence and with a narrow needle of guilty awareness that this was all just the way Ted had liked it on the side.

They went out to his black Bel Air in the driveway before the silence was broken. Yes, they'd exchanged small pleasantries over their food or when he opened the car door for her but the first statement with any actual meaning was:

"How do you know where to find him, this 'funny little man.'"

"I guess I don't know. I mean, I suppose everybody knows. He keeps to himself on a little dirt road outside of town, but he's been there as long as anyone can remember."

Holyoak wondered at that, realized that he was scowling at her and tried to soften his face. "Let's see," he said as he rolled the ignition over.

It was true somehow. The shack *did* look like one of those places that everybody knew about but nobody noticed. There was something in the air around it that Holyoak didn't like, some outré and tingling sensation that could only be magic. He found it difficult to believe that this guy hadn't been noticed by the Sabremen or that he didn't know about their true purpose.

As he drew closer, he realized that "shack" wasn't really the right word. It wasn't a nice place, but it was hardly a hovel. The grounds were unkempt and the house in disrepair with chipping paint and broken shingles, but it was more that it gave off the impression on some unconscious level of eldritch and decaying energy.

Mrs. Clark knocked softly. After an impatient moment, Holyoak knocked more robustly. There were sounds of shuffling for a moment before the door opened.

"Yes?" came a weak voice. Holyoak was taken aback. Mrs. Clark had described a "funny little man," and while the description was strictly accurate, the tweedy, balding, bespectacled man in the sweater vest standing in the doorway was not what he expected.

"Good morning," Holyoak said, suddenly aware of the briskness of the wind. "I'm Rev. Holyoak. I think you may know Mrs. Clark."

The little man looked rapidly between their faces. "Yes, yes. I'm Professor Llewyn. Come in. We haven't much time."

The house was packed with books, most old, a few new and all very strange. They had overflowed the sagging bookcases and seemed to pile unevenly on every flat surface. Hanging from the far wall was a golden sculpture of a seated figure in a cowled robe, enshrined in beams of radiance, an indecipherable slogan etched in hooked letters around the circumference. Holyoak's suspicions regarding the amulet were confirmed: the professor was a Lengite, though more intellectual and less barbarically strange than most.

The professor moved some books from the chairs in his living room, and Holyoak caught a glimpse of some of the titles: *Nameless Cults*, *Ancient Weird Religious Rites*, a snakeskin-bound *The King in Yellow*. He saw a copy of *The Fault in Our Stars* by Dr. Herbert Llewyn and realized that he recognized the name of their host. He had been a well-known but ultimately discredited professor of astronomy at Arizona State, removed from his post for his increasingly radical insistence on intertwining magic and mythology with hard science.

Politely, Joanne sat, disturbing the dust in the chair and Holyoak followed her lead. "Alright professor. I'm aware of your work—and your reputation. Normally I'm patient, as a man of the cloth should be, but something's got this town's Sabreman lodge under its heel and their women too. God help me, I don't even know what happening to the children while their mothers run around like feral killers and their fathers madly worship that devil-woman-thing—"

"Khalimak," the professor said coolly.

"I suppose that's some Lengite goddess?" Holyoak's voice was low and grave.

The professor smiled wryly, at last sitting down in what was apparently his own regular perch as it was filled with neither books nor dust. Joanne was out of her depth and the expression on her face made it plain. If she'd picked up his comment about her girlfriends, she was keeping her reaction muted.

"Lengites believe in Khalimak's existence. They do not worship her. She is an evil power, to be shunned and avoided. It was she whom Victoria's armies confused with the Hindoo mother goddess, she who ruled over the murdering thugs in the mountains and highways of South Asia. It is she now who corrupts this place, for her love is poison and her womanhood vileness. But both are irresistible."

"But you knew this would happen," Holyoak leaned menacingly over the arm of his chair, pointed at the amulet at Joanne's neck. "You gave her that. Why?"

"I suspected that something had gone awry when the Sabremen brought that idol back from one of their... adventures. But I had no way of knowing if it was merely an image of Khalimak or a true focus for her presence."

Holyoak was seething now. He half rose, gripping the little man by his collar. "You're involved in this somehow. I know it!"

The professor's small eyes were wide open with panic. "You've seen her! This is her influence!"

Holyoak stepped back, dropping the little man back into his chair. "Their idols are silver and gold, the work of men's hands. They have mouths, but they speak not: eyes have they, but they see not—"

"I fear Khalimak's do. And her hands may handle not, and her feet may walk not, but her strength is great and her reach long."

"What do we do?" Joanne asked, breaking her long silence. "This is all very interesting, but what do we do about it?"

"We can't go in fighting." Holyoak felt tired as he spoke, settling into his seat again. "People who are really innocent will get hurt."

"Agreed," Llewyn nodded.

"Won't this help?" Joanne asked, holding up the necklace.

"That's a powerful token," Llewyn mused, "but it only provided some resistance. You haven't gone mad, but tell me, have you been feeling yourself?"

Joanne blushed, looking down and biting her lip—hard. "I've been feeling... urges."

"That will only continue—for both of you, until you become like the rest of them."

"Why haven't you been effected?" Holyoak asked.

"My home is safe, under the protection of elder gods. If you stayed here long enough the effects you are already feeling would dissipate."

"That's not why we're here." Holyoak gritted his teeth.

"I know," the professor sighed. "There is a rite we can perform, but we will have to get close enough to the statue to bind it in cords of pure silver—which we will have to make unless you have access to some."

"There was a chain like that at the Lodge," Holyoak remembered. "They must have used it to transport her."

"And someone must have removed it," the professor sighed again. "An easy idea for Khalimak to have planted in a weak enough mind."

The professor began to rummage around, finding a particular slim volume of spells and a handled hook of some golden metal that looked almost like a blunted scythe. "We must prepare. I will invoke the elder gods and…"

"You do that," Holyoak said, holding up his hand. "My trust is in the Lord.

"We'll meet you there."

III

IT WAS midday when they converged on the Sabremen lodge. Joanne had ridden with Holyoak of course, and they found Llewyn already there, tangled in hand-to-hand combat with one of those feral housewives. Valiantly, the little man fought the amazon with the molting beehive and the broken heels as she strove to drive her steak knife into his throat. He struck her in the side of the face with that curious golden scythe and she crumpled to ground with a yelp, before slinking away into the brush like a kicked puppy.

"This way!" he whispered sibilantly, motioned them towards the door.

It was much the same scene as when Holyoak had been there before, only more worn-down and desperate. The lodge brothers lay in piles, propped up against each others' backs, still twitching rhythmically to an eerie drone that seemed to emanate from the very walls.

From the edges and corners of the room, the wild women slowly crept. Holyoak had drawn the great guns from beneath his coat, but the ammo clattered harmlessly in his pockets—though it was there, just in case. He held the guns by their barrels blunted tools of violence that would hopefully at least defend him from these mindless attackers—would at least allow him to defend Joanne.

With surprising speed and aggression, Llewyn leapt into the fray, brandishing his eldritch weapon and sending two of the women aside in blind panic. Beside Holyoak, Joanne was seized by rough hands, their ruby nails like claws in her flesh. To her surprise, she found herself hissing, scratching madly at the woman's face, pushing her down and drawing twin streams of dark blood.

"Hurry, Xavier," she said. "I don't think we have much time."

Llewyn's luck had run out: he had two of the beastly women on him now, and a third was approaching. Holyoak jumped towards them, smashing the butt of a revolver against her brow. It would be a hell of a bruise, but she'd be fine if any of them were… if they could just get through this.

Llewyn yelped, and Holyoak looked to see him, still beset by two attackers. A long knife twisted mostly harmlessly against the sweater vest that had been better armor than any would have guessed, but blood was being drawn. Holyoak repositioned his hands on the barrels of the mighty guns and prepared to launch again into action.

"No!" Llewyn shouted. "Get to the idol!"

Holyoak sprung the other way, bounding past the emaciated bodies of the Sabremen towards the dais. He felt just about to make it when he hit that shimmering field around the statue itself. He felt as if he was moving through mud, hit by wave after wave of nausea, dizziness, and something akin to the intense effects of lustful arousal with every hint of the pleasure removed. He crumpled to the floor. He realized that the droning sound was no longer a single note, but a rhythm that the whole world was moving to.

Looking up, he saw the framed portraits of the men who had served as the lodge's Sergeants-at-Arms. Ted's picture was among them. He saw Joanne, her back to him, staring at it in the middle of the mad scene all around her. She went up to it, stroked the still image of Ted's face. Then she turned resolutely towards the altar.

A snarling woman leapt into her path, but Joanne, calmly this time, merely seized her by her pearl necklace and threw her to one side, the pearls clattering on the floor beneath them.

Holyoak watched as she stooped to pick up the silver chain at the idol's feet and began to drape it over its four spread arms. The noise and sickness started to leave him immediately, but Llewyn was first to run up beside her, still bleeding from his side, and help her bind the cord more tightly.

Holyoak rose up on one side and surveyed the damage. The lodge was a shambles. The housewives, as if waking up from a nightmare hungover, had begun to cry. Some were moving to their husbands, who conversely, had slipped into the most exhausted of sleeps. Joanne helped the limping professor to a seat, and Holyoak, watching, knew that the trinket at her throat had been useless.

The pure love between her and her husband had protected her, and for a time, had protected him, even if its friction against Khalimak's power had ultimately driven him to insanity and death. She had found that, deep in her grief at the moment it counted most. And he knew what he had known deep down since coming here and falling a little under her spell. Now that this was over, he'd be moving on.

IV

"WE CAN'T thank you enough Reverend for all of your help." Nelson Smith was the lodge's mage—the leader of this particular group. He was dressed for convalescence, in a smoking jacket and slippers but his fez was very much back on his head.

"We do what we can for each other," Holyoak said shaking his hand. "Is that idol still here?"

"We've arranged to have it moved to where it can be better… cared for." Smith said dryly. "We're very lucky. The kids and the elderly relatives of our lodge brothers seem to have been held in some kind of stasis. That Llewyn fellow seemed to think it was more important to Khalimak to keep from making a scene and being exposed to the community at large until her foothold here was really established."

"Thank God," Holyoak said. "Where is Llewyn?"

"Still in the hospital" Joanne interjected.

"He did ask us to give you this letter," Smith said, handing him an envelope with no inscription. "It's from a mutual friend who needs our help, which we are obviously in no shape to give at the moment. Llewyn suggested you and I couldn't think of anyone better."

Holyoak smiled a small, rough smile, nodding his head.

Smith doubled over, a flash of pain crossing his face. He excused himself, apologizing for not letting them out.

"What will you do now?" Joanne—Mrs. Clark—asked expectantly.

"I'll look into this, I suppose," he said indicating the letter as he moved it to his pocket.

"Will you stay tonight, at least?"

He looked into those sad, waiting eyes, and felt the weight of his mission on his heart.

"No. I'm headed out, as soon as I collect my things."

"Well, don't stay too late. There will be a lot of traffic coming into town later for that women's wrestling match tonight."

Holyoak chuckled. After everything he'd been through, that sounded especially ridiculous.

"I'll see you back at the house, then," Joanne said, turning to go. "I'll make sure everything is ready."

"Joanne," Holyoak said as she stepped through the door. Her eyes lit up and she smiled. Was that the first time he had called her by her first name? "For what it's worth, I wish I could stay… Ted… was very lucky to have you."

"I know," she smiled. "Both things."

She closed the door between them.

Outing to Nowhere

I

THEY HAD set off first thing in the morning under heavy cloud cover, driving down the twisting two-lane blacktop as it snaked through the mountains and darting through banks of fog that clung to the earth, jealous of their celestial brethren.

"Let me see that telegram again," Rev. Holyoak said, turning to the powerfully built woman sitting next to him. She handed him the note, giving him a quick chance to accidentally look at her legs. She was a lot of woman this one. In the ring, they called her the B. F. M., the Blunt Force Mama. She hadn't told him her real name, so he called her "B." She didn't seem to mind. She looked out of place with her massive, steely body in that long sleeved, short dress with her wide shoulders bare. She was every bit a woman, although there was enough of her for two. Holyoak's white collar started to itch, as it often did when he felt his lust rising, and he stretched it away from his neck before looking down at the note:

AZ SR16 KEEP DRIVING COME QUICKLY
MR P

The first and most obvious problem with this was that there wasn't a State Route 16 in Arizona. A worse problem was that they had just found it, right where the self-styled "half-breed shaman" on the Reservation had said it would be, his smile wicked and reeking of days of heavy drinking. The sign was old and rusty, "State Route 16" emblazoned along with a swastika-marked arrowhead within the shape of the state.

"I don't like this, Xavier" said B., her Texan voice, as big as the rest of her, filling the car.

"It's okay. The Indians used that symbol too. It's just a coincidence. All the signs out here looked like that before the War."

"That's not what I mean and you know it," she pouted uncharacteristically. "That symbol means power. It marks this place as a crossroads."

Holyoak nodded silently as they turned past the sign and onto the route. They drove in silence for a while. He started to feel something uncomfortable as if they were being watched. His steel-blue eyes darted along the roadside and he took notice of an unusual number of black birds perched on nearby rocks as the road became narrower between the mountains. And there still hadn't been a break in the clouds. They seemed heavy, darker, and low, as if they meant to smother them in the narrowing road.

B.'s nails bit into his arm. "Xavier! They're everywhere!"

He pulled his arm away, irritably. "What're ya yelling for? They're just birds! When did you become such a waif?"

She retreated, hurt. It wasn't like her to be so soft and timid. And it wasn't like him to be so brusque. Truth was he felt those birds with their shining eyes pressing on him, felt the ride get tighter with every mountain turn. He focused straight ahead on the road, taking off his collar and putting it between them, pulling at his shirt to cool his neck.

"Look," he said. "I'm sorry. This place is giving me the creeps too. But it's just birds, I'm sure—" Suddenly a great black bird smashed into the windshield, spattering its blood and brains and dung in front of them before its corpse tumbled over the car. Holyoak swerved, almost missing the sharp turn that took them into the next valley. The tires squealed, Holyoak grunting as he struggled to hold the wheel. The shriek continued after he righted the car and he realized B. was still screaming. She caught herself and looked away embarrassed, her dark, Jane Russell hairdo bobbing as she turned her head. It was even darker in this valley, the clouds were still heavy, but it should have been morning still if not noon and it was as dark as dusk. Holyoak nudged B.

"It looks like you were right to get spooked."

They were descending into a wide valley and the mountains rolled on before, crowding the horizon. She looked forward through the windshield, craning her neck to see the sky. A great swirl of black birds was revolving in the sky like a galaxy being born in the darkness. They drove on.

"Must you drum your fingers like that?" B. asked, an edge in her voice. Holyoak emerged from his reverie, stopping the beating motion of his fingers against the steering wheel. He let out an audible sigh from behind gritted teeth.

"We'll need to stop for gas soon," he said, eyeing the gauge curiously. The gas tank should have been empty a long time ago. B. said nothing. Holyoak impatiently swept back a few stray hairs and kept driving, his nerves tingling with irritation. An exit sign appeared on the horizon. The sky was the same shade of cloudy gray it had been for the last few hours, but as he got closer, he could make it out:

WELCOME TO PROSPECT
EXIT ON SCATTERBRAIN LANE

The words "NO GAS" were crudely painted underneath. Nonetheless, he steered the car towards the exit.

"Why are we stopping here, Xavier? It says there's no gas anyway."

"It's the first sign of anything we've seen for hours, B." he said, tightening his square jaw and trying hard to swallow the bite in his voice as the tires ground against the dirt road of Scatterbrain Lane. They rode past the remains of a burned down trailer, its more solid parts standing up like the ribs of a great animal carcass. Feral cats, huge and hairy, watched them from the wreck with shining eyes.

"Xavier..." she started to say.

"Hush! The gas station's right ahead. We can at least find out where the next town is before we slink off like scared children," he responded forcibly, feeling a little rush at treating such a rare woman so commandingly. He immediately felt ashamed. B. turned to the window, stiff and silent.

A young man in a shabby attendant's uniform emerged from the little gas station as their wheels ground to a stop. He was tall and thin and Holyoak had to admit that he gave him a tinge of primal discomfort to look at. His eyes were just a little too far apart and although it was darkening, his acne-scarred skin looked the wrong shade of green for a healthy human being.

"No gas, mister," he shouted running towards the car. He stopped, seeing B., and started giggling uncontrollably. "Oh, hiyah missus. We don't see too many ladies around here. I don't mean to be starin'."

B. turned back, scowled at him, and then continued her ruminations on whatever lay beyond the window. Despite his protestations, the attendant, who was named "Obi" or was wearing Obi's clothes, continued to lean into the window, staring at B. Holyoak liked the smell of him even less than his looks.

"Listen, Obi is it?"

Obi nodded.

"Obi, I know you don't have any gas here, but I was hoping you could tell me where the nearest real town was, someplace where we could get something to eat and fill up."

"I don't know much about any other towns nearby excepting Prospect," Obi said, thoughtfully rubbing his chin. "I got a phone you can use, but I don't know who you'd call."

"That's fine, Obi," Holyoak said, opening his door without giving the lad much time to get away, and taking his collar from the bench seat next to him.

Obi led the way into the store, looking back briefly just as Holyoak was working the stiff white collar into his shirt. He seemed to sneer uncomfortably, but quickly laughed it off. "Sorry," he said, "we get even fewer reverends than we do pretty ladies out here."

"It's okay son, if I could just use your phone."

"Yes, mist— reverend that is, it's right through here." Obi pushed open a tattered screen door that couldn't have kept out one of the wild cats they'd seen, let alone an errant insect, and indicated an old-style wall telephone. Picking it up, Holyoak heard a few loud clicks and then a labored wheezing that sounded unearthly over the poor line.

"Hello, operator?" he asked unsurely.

"How can I connect you?" came the reply, sounding far away and warbling like no sound from a human mouth could. Surely a bad connection.

"I'm passing through and I was hoping you could direct me to the nearest town with gas."

"Hold please." The voice was labored and thick.

Holyoak absently looked around. Every wall was covered in tacky knick-knacks: Gimmicky animal heads, like a jackalope, a two-headed Gila and other things he didn't recognize. A couple of overlapping pin-ups near the phone caught his attention, and he looked through them. At least these seemed normal enough, except for the disturbing, handwritten captions that boldly implied their author's unusual tastes. He noticed that there was a calendar behind them and moved them aside, spinning them on their tacks. A nude photo adorned the calendar, a lithe, green-skinned beauty with a typically surprised expression, kneeling and demurely pressing her three bosoms together. Miss Reapingmoon 1958. The 8th, 16th, and 40th days of Reapingmoon were marked on the calendar with arcane symbols.

Before he could decide what he thought of this unearthly artifact of earthy passions, a clatter came from behind the counter where Obi stood, straining to catch another look a B. through his window. Awkwardly, he gathered up the oil cans and other detritus that he had scattered carelessly to the floor. Holyoak turned at the commotion, and as he turned back to the phone, spotted an ornate fez proudly displayed on a nearby table. He recognized the style, and placed the phone's receiver aside. The fez was marked with the image of a long, curved sword and with the words "Mn. ADEPT" in rhinestones: A Silver Sabreman's ceremonial headgear. He picked it up and saw a ring of dried blood staining the inside.

"Hey, don't touch that!" Obi said, noticing that Holyoak had moved away from the phone and trying to get around the mess behind the counter to stop him.

Holyoak bolted for the door, waving his arms wildly at B. as he passed the threshold. She was standing by the car door looking at her surroundings in the eerie, ambient half-light. She sprang into action as soon as she saw him, not the timid driving companion of the day but the fighter that Holyoak knew her to be. She picked up a crate from near the car, lifting it over her head with her thick arms and launching it past him to strike down Obi just as he emerged from the shop, a jagged, rusty dagger in his hand. Obi fell to the ground with a grunt, the dagger clattering on the wooden porch.

The scrape of rubber against the dirt road awoke Obi from where he lay, and he muttered a curse in some forgotten language at them as they sped away back into the unknown.

They had been speeding into the night for some time before Rev. Holyoak relaxed his foot on the gas. The night was dark and cloudless and something that he couldn't make out was wrong with the stars. Beside him, B. sat dozing. Her breath was even and calm and that filled him with quiet rage. He spoke aloud, pretending not to realize she was sleeping.

"I think I have some idea where we are," he said flatly, squinting at the peculiar stars. B. came to, looking around. "Nice of you to join us," he said with an icy edge in his voice.

"I'm sorry, Xavier" she said, stretching her long, muscular arms. He ducked away dramatically, scowling. "Gee," she said, crossing her arms, "I'm sorry." Her voice was sarcastic, but there was a hint of real hurt there too. He thrilled at it for an instant before the bitter taste of self-loathing uncoiled in his gut.

He straightened out. "It's alright," he said guiltily, craning his neck at the unfamiliar constellations. "None of these stars are right," he said under his breath, like a curse.

"What gives?" she asked. "I thought you said you knew where we were."

"I said I had *an idea* where we are." The road veered suddenly and he did curse as he pulled the car tightly around the bend, tires squealing as the headlights cast their dancing pools across the barren road and the rocky crags on either side of them. B. dug her nails into his arm. A feminine gesture, but with her strength a horrible press of spikes, tearing his jacket, shirt and flesh. He wheeled around, hand up as if to strike her and in that split second saw not terror, but wild malice in her eyes. She pelted the side of his face with the back of her hand, his world momentarily encapsulated in the dull thud of his head bouncing off the driver's side window. He slammed the brakes, a cloud of dust filling the headlights in front of them.

"I wasn't going to hit you," he said. He felt as much like crying as he ever had, as if every bum rap of his life had come back to him at once.

"You should have!" she spat back, she was splayed out in the seat and against the door, like an animal about to pounce. "I deserve to be punished! If God wants to punish me through one of his servants than it's only right!" She rolled her head back, great tears escaping her eyes.

"I'm no man of God!" he whimpered. "I've loved women, got a kick out of the power of righteousness I'm a fraud B., a fraud!" He had reached across to her, was shaking her. She was becoming hysterical.

"You don't understand," she moaned. "I couldn't give up my life. I knew what I was doing when I got in the ring that night, I knew what would happen!" He was holding her now, holding on for her or for himself – he couldn't be sure. "I couldn't be a mother, couldn't bring a child into my world, I couldn't—"

"A world like this one," he said, his eyes bulging, his teeth gritted. "Filled with men like me who claim to follow the light while crawling in darkness." Over her shoulder he saw the sun rising through her window, like no sun he had ever seen. A thin circle of light like a permanent eclipse, flaring sharply but bringing no brightness or color to the inky blackness in sky, and casting the landscape in sharp relief where it touched it.

"God has abandoned us, Xavier," she said looking into his eyes, her wide shoulders shivering.

Holyoak felt himself sink into the lowest depths of feeling, but there he found a spark, something which rang defiant against her words. "No!" he shouted, shaking her again, her hair tousling about her face. "Never!"

He became calm again. "B., it's this place. I had thought it before but now I know." Her body relaxed and she sat back in her seat, eyeing him suspiciously. "The Silver Sabremen believe in a place they call 'the Gloaming' that runs alongside our world like the deep currents of a river that looks calm. They say it can be reached by any number of byways."

She was interested, and her skeptical look was better than the suspicion and fear of a moment ago. "Or highways?" she asked.

He nodded and continued, gesticulating wildly: "The Gloaming is like our world but it's broken. It's dangerous. Even top adepts in the Sabremen are fearful of it."

"It was the Sabremen who gave you this assignment, wasn't it?" she asked.

He nodded. "And it was the fez of a Sabreman, kept as a trophy, that alerted me to danger back in Prospect."

"So you think we're in this 'Gloaming?'" she asked, calm but still incredulous.

"Does that look like the sun to you?" he asked, gesturing out the window behind her.

She gasped. "But Xavier..."

"It's this place, B. It turned us against each other and then against ourselves. I had always assumed that it was a metaphor, like so much of their kooky religion, but I look at that abomination hanging in the sky and—" He took her hand. "God hasn't abandoned us, B. And I'll stick with you if stick with me."

She smiled, her grip tight on his hand, and wiped away a tear from either eye. "Let's keep going, I think I saw lights in the valley before we stopped here. Maybe we can find a place to regroup and... I'm starved, Xavier." She smiled.

"Me, too," he said, smiling himself as he put the car back into drive and slowly pulled onto the road again.

They had seen lights in the valley, although it was only a solitary shack, casting long, bright rectangles from its front door and windows. A line of twisted, gleaming shapes was parked along the side: hotrods, but not based on any model they had ever seen back in what they were coming to think of as the "real world." The lines of the chrome on each of these unique rides was glinting in the light of a neon sign that read "EAT AT AZOG'S."

Holyoak parked the car away from the others, in a patch that was darker even than the rest of their surroundings. Cautiously, they got out of the car and walked to the bright light of the doorway. It looked like a typical diner inside, or rather like dope fiend's dream of one. The attendant at the counter squinted curiously at them as they entered. He was dressed in a sickly green apron and sweat-stained paper hat. All the physical attributes they had seen in the gas station attendant back in Prospect were pronounced here: His skin was definitely green and his eyes were decidedly too far apart. Something in his look made Holyoak glad he had put his collar in his pocket on the way in.

Seated at the booths were all manner of misproportioned guests, all dressed for a night on the town. At one table was a group of men with over-wide mouths and low brows. Each seemed subtly a different shade of unhealthy: one blue, one pink, one as green as their friend at the counter, but their hair was greased back in flawless pompadours and they wore well-ironed, matching bowling shirts with bats embroidered on them. When B. stepped into the diner behind Holyoak, they smiled lasciviously at her, revealing how full those wide mouths were of sharpened teeth. One licked his eyebrow smooth before leaving his long tongue hanging out of his mouth. B. glared calmly back, straightening her dress beneath her as she sat at the bar, her back to them. Holyoak smiled as he sat down next to her. He was glad to see her be herself again.

The attendant approached them, still trying to measure them up. "What'll have?"

Holyoak looked up at the menu on the chalkboard behind the waiter. It was covered in eldritch runes he couldn't read and in strange names that he couldn't understand. "What's good tonight?" he asked.

"How about a grenburger?" B. interjected. "That seems normal enough."

"Between you and me," the server said, leaning in. "Not so fresh right now. The gren's almost dead and the meat's getting tough." B. gulped hard and turned away. Holyoak wasn't sure if it was the description of the food or the smell of the attendant that put her off. It wasn't that he smelled *bad* exactly, he just didn't have that subtle smell of *people* that you never notice unless it's off.

A small man in tweed approached the counter. "They'll have the felb salad I think, Hiram." The little man insinuated himself between their stools. Holyoak nodded and the waiter went to the back. "It's the least offensive thing on the menu I think you'll find. My name is Mr. Nizbert, and I do hope you won't judge the local food based on Azog's cooking." His smile was pronouncedly crooked to left and his hand was cold and clammy as he gingerly took theirs. "You are Mr. Phillips' associates, I take it?"

Holyoak nodded. "Do you have something for us?"

The waiter emerged with two cracked salad bowls full of chucks of spiny succulents and something brown and gelatinous. B. dug in, concern marking her face until replaced by relief after the first chews. Holyoak followed suit. It wasn't bad. It wasn't good either.

Mr. Nizbert had been cleaning has glasses, and now produced a note from his tweed jacket. The envelope was marked "Rev. Holyoak." The attendant saw it and his eyes widened.

"You're the Reverend Holyoak?" he asked, anger and fear in his voice.

At this the monstrous bowling team behind them took notice, leaving their table and surrounding them at the counter. A big one, the leader, put his hand on Holyoak's shoulder. "We know you. You're the one they call 'God's Hitman.'" Holyoak looked at B., who stopped chewing and changed her grip on her fork. Mr. Nizbert inched away, quietly.

"Hey, Bugba, I think maybe we should show our friends outside," the creature, the green one holding him said, drawing a laugh from his friends. B. spun around knocking one of their assailants back and jamming her fork awkwardly into another's gut—the pink one—producing pinpricks of blood on his immaculate bowling shirt, directly below where "Bugba" was embroidered. He quickly stepped back and reviewed the damage.

"Now that's gonna stain!" he shouted, his voice low and gravelly, the bone through his nose wobbling as his nostrils flared with rage. He started at B., expecting to scare her, but she took two steps forward instead, her heels clicking methodically on the floorboards, and belted him square between the eyes with a left cross. Bugba fell drooling as his friends attacked in force, three against two. Holyoak put up his dukes, backing against the bar—behind which the attendant crouched, whimpering—and fending off two at once, the orange and the green who seemed to be the leader of the pack. B. made two smooth sweeps at the legs of the blue one, drawing out the space between them. Holyoak couldn't keep his eyes off those long, muscular legs of hers, and it was fortunate that he wasn't the only one: He finally got an opening and pelted the leader repeatedly in the face with a series of well-timed, rabbit-fast punches that dropped him cross-eyed. B. meanwhile leapt onto a nearby table and launched herself at her opponent, pinning him down and holding her fork to his throat. Holyoak's other opponent held up his hands with a shrug. His shirt said "Runt." It seemed appropriate.

"Let's go B." Holyoak said. She lifted herself slowly off of her fallen foe, who was starting to look like he was enjoying himself. He let out a long whistle as he watched her go, causing her to turn back and shoot the fork at him, leaving it vibrating with a twang in the floorboards an inch from his head.

Mr. Nizbert approached the pair as they reached the door. "You should go quickly, before their boss gets here." He urged them out with a hand on each of their backs. "You'll meet Mr. Phillips at the Monastery of Leng. Read the letter on the road—it will guide you the rest of the way—and for Dagon's sake cover up! There's a moonquake coming."

The night air was still as they walked back to the car. The shadow of "Runt" darkened the doorway. "Yeah, y—you better leave!" he stuttered. "The Clipper'll take care of you!"

Their eyes adjusted as they approached the car. A tall shape stood over it. Holyoak's first impression was of the sort of "wolf" cartoon that you might see in a girlie mag: wrinkled suit, crumpled top hat and all.

"Nice wheels, brother." Came the voice, smooth and very low. "What is it?" The question was sincerely posed. His hairy hands ran over the lines of the car.

"It's a '57 Bel Air." Holyoak responded defensively.

"You know, I hear what sounds like a couple of roughs messing up my boys, but I smell a woman!" The figure laughed maniacally as he turned. The face was the fanged and snouted face of a wolf, but a single bulging eye rolled about in the center of its forehead. He threw his head back and howled at the sky. A great gold necklace—the word "Clipper"—glinted in the light of Azog's neon sign.

Just then the ground heaved, and the thin ring of light that stood for the sun widened on one side, casting harsh shine and deep shadow on the knotty, twisted and thorny, cactus-like plants that dotted the landscape. The Clipper covered his face with his hairy paws, but B. and Holyoak's unprotected skin seemed to blister and smoke instantly. B. ran to the driver's door on the other side of the car, while the enraged Clipper tossed Holyoak around by his lapels. B. turned the key and backed the car away from the scene, leaving the passenger's seat towards him.

"Get in!" she shouted, opening the passenger door as she saw a momentary break in the tussle. Holyoak sprinted towards the car and rolled into the bench seat. B. was off before he had the door closed, the silhouette of the Clipper filling the rear-view mirror as he watched them, howling at the wavering moon in rage.

Holyoak scrambled in the glove compartment, producing two pairs of driving gloves and two pairs of sunglasses. "What is this?" B. screamed, tearing two lengths of fabric from her dress, and wrapping one around her face before handing the other to him.

"I don't know," he said, covering his face and hands and giving B. the extra pairs. "Some kind of radiation if I had to guess."

"Monster bowlers, the big bad wolf, and a radioactive sun?" she said with a smirk that Holyoak could hear in her voice. "Tell me again about this Gloaming theory."

There was a sharp dip in the road and B. had to swerve to compensate.

"Careful..." Holyoak said.

"Worried about your car?" B. asked, that same smirk in her voice. "Don't you trust me?"

"I trust you, B." he said, a smile in his own voice. "I trust you."

11

THEY HAD followed the instructions in Mr. Phillips' letter, part roadmap and part sigil. They took roads that lead to nowhere, into open plains that were valleys when they entered them and across mountains lit only by eerie lights flashing in the sky. Great planetary spheres winked out from cloud cover and then failed to reemerge when the clouds passed over them. The radioactive sun had set, and a crimson red dawn was coming up slowly from the horizon. They crossed a long and ancient stone bridge which looked older than mankind, but which was nonetheless paved with the striped blacktop. There, on a vast plateau it stood, an imposing and ancient structure. B.'s nails bit into the steering wheel. She slowed the car to a crawl, the tires grinding on the pavement. Holyoak had let her drive, meaning that it was he who had read the letter, giving the directions in the few places where the road had diverged, and he who had spoken aloud the elemental watchwords and incantations. He felt strange. Not like he had sinned exactly, but that he had done something—touched some power—that he shouldn't have. He'd replaced his white collar and was somehow reassured by it.

He considered telling B. that it looked like a straight shot across the bridge and that time was of the essence, but looking out the window he couldn't see the bottom of the chasm they were over, only darkness.

B. stared in awe at the massive edifice before them. "I always assumed the Monastery of Leng was in China," she said, almost to herself.

"Look around B." he said. "I don't think we're anywhere near China, or Arizona, or Kansas for that matter." Holyoak caught a flicker of red fire over the horizon. "Be careful, B." he said. "But dawn is coming, and I don't think it's a dawn we want to see. She pressed slightly harder on the gas, until at last they rolled the car to the colossal iron gates. A yellow-robed and hooded monk approached them, peering into the window as Holyoak rolled it down. He had drawn, satyric features, his skin the color and texture of old parchment. Holyoak held up Mr. Phillips' letter, and B. saw enough of it through the back of the translucent paper to make her glad she had kept her eyes on the road. The monk bowed his head, casting his large, goat's eyes down as he backed away. With a sound like an earthquake, coming as from deep below, the chains strained and the iron gate slowly lifted.

They rolled into the courtyard, stopping before a titanic, dried-up fountain festooned with gargoyles. They rose from the car and looked around. The architecture was not quite Oriental—more like a Spanish monk's nightmare of China. They found themselves squinting in a light that was growing brighter in the reddening sky. The monk who had granted them entrance came running towards them, shielding himself with his robes.

"Come!" he shouted in a high, thin voice, motioning them on as he made for the shelter of the arches beyond. They followed him into the shadows and he continued as they approached: "The day is not safe." He pulled a chain in front of the arched door and a great bellows sounded before the door creaked open and an identical monk ushered them inside. The monks led them through from the great hall and through stone corridors, walking briskly past hideous, demonic gods housed in ornate alcoves and without greeting their fellows, who were occupied with hastily drawing massive, heavy drapes across every window.

They passed over a large chamber, with a ring of stone altars, all caked with dark, splattered stains. B. shuddered visibly. Holyoak didn't blame her, but he kept his cool, knowing they were being watched curiously—and led purposefully to somewhere in the dark and eerie abbey.

At last they came to a set of ornately carved wooden doors. The monks stood on either side and pushed the doors open with a bow. They remained bent, and Holyoak and B. hesitantly entered the room—a vast library crammed floor to ceiling with tomes, some with leather so new that it still looked wet, others nearly crumbling to dust. The monks closed the doors behind them, silent except for the final, loud click as they met. A fire burned low and red behind a blackened grate, a lone figure beside it dressed in a suit that was all black but which was perfectly ordinary. He lowered and closed the book which hid his face. His features were gaunt, his hair gray, but his eyes twinkled with the dim light of one who has scrutinized the world and found it wanting.

"Mr. Phillips, I presume?" Holyoak asked as they approached. Phillips extended his hand. Holyoak found it soft and warm and somehow reassuring after the strangeness they had been mired in for the last few days. He found himself silently wondering if it had been days, hours or years since they set out. "Reverend Xavier Holyoak," he managed. Phillips nodded, withdrawing his hand and rising to his almost six feet to make an awkward greeting as Holyoak introduced "B." Though his hair was gray and his skin wrinkled and thin, his true age was only revealed in the crookedness of the man's stance.

"So," he said suddenly. "I suppose you two are the Sabremen's answer to the cavalry." His voice was higher and thinner than expected for a man of his size and presence, and despite carrying what sounded like an affectation of limey, was undoubtedly New England underneath.

"Something like that," Holyoak said coolly, still trying to size the man up. "I thought you'd be expecting us."

"My associate, one Mr. Nizbert, was entrusted to make arrangements," Phillips said. "A strange and subhuman being, but I find him to be trustworthy."

"Look," Holyoak began, "the truth is..."

"Truth is," B. interjected, "we don't really know why we're here. We were just given your message and told to come get you."

"I see," Phillips gravely nodded his head. "Best to start at the beginning." Phillips looked out and his voice, previously thin and high took on the command of narration. "I have taken refuge in this place for many years, studying these old and eldritch tomes that I surround myself with, plumbing the depths of the secret worlds all around us." He smiled bitterly. "And yet I find doors still closed to me, texts—one in particular—which the High Priest of this place refuses to let me read. What starry wisdom it contains I can only guess at, for though it sits in the weird sanctuary of this place it is always watched."

"You brought us here—wherever here is—because this priest wouldn't punch your library card?" B. leaned in menacingly. He did not flinch.

"You misunderstand me, madam." He said, command still in his voice. "This is not some petty quest for intellectual baubles. The knowledge contained is this tome may spell the difference between the cosmos as we understand it and blind, inchoate darkness, for there are dark and ancient forces at play that crave the same hidden formulas of this ancient science—and science it is, despite—" he gestured to the antique, moldering room around them, "—the trappings. One such player in this mad game—a monstrous and subhuman mongrel, a gangster who calls himself 'the Clipper'—has had his lackeys searching for this place for decades." He noticed Holyoak and B. exchange a look between them. "You know of him then?"

"We've had that distasteful experience, yes," Holyoak nodded.

"He didn't get the scent of you, did he?" Phillips asked, his face drawn.

"He got mine," B. sighed.

"This is very grave," Phillips said, his voice returning to its less imposing default. "There is little we shall be able to do during the day, but the Clipper's 'men' will not be able to approach under the red sun either."

"You mean, he's followed us here?" B. asked. "But why didn't he just take the road all this time?"

"A road that goes nowhere..." Holyoak began.

"Can go anywhere." Phillips finished. "Without a map like the one my diminutive associate gave you, it would be nearly impossible to reach this place. But a definite scent for the Clipper's lycanthropic snout to follow is just as good. He'll be here as soon as darkness permits." He breathed deeply. "Come, we must speak to the High Priest of this." Despite his stature and age, he sped past them, only a slight hobble in his gate, not even holding the door for them as he left the room with them in tow.

"Do not look directly at the High Priest," Phillips began as they approached the gilt sanctuary.

"Not exactly that old time religion, then?" Holyoak asked.

Phillips stopped and looked him in the eye for the first time. "Do not look at the High Priest directly because you will not like the effect he has on your eyes. While witch doctors of your ilk" he gestured at Holyoak's collar "make great claims to the masses, the High Priest here is truly of another world." He turned and began to lead them again. "Look too closely and you will learn why they call him the Indescribable One."

Their footsteps echoed as they approached the sanctuary, passing loathsome, cracking frescoes on the walls which seemed to depict every form of massacre and atrocity known or unknown to man. As they approached a yawning alcove of pitch blackness they walked past the dark-stained ring of stone altars they had seen before, and saw an abysmal well between them. Off to the side, two goatish monks, much larger than the others, bearded and with great, bare chests stood on either side of an enshrined book, armed with wicked, curved and hooked swords. Phillips eyed the book hungrily as they passed and Holyoak saw that the guards did not notice. As they drew closer, he saw why: their empty eye sockets had been crudely sewn shut, but they seemed nonetheless tense, poised to attack, and very much aware of their presence.

Holyoak began to sense a high and trembling whine that he realized he had been hearing for a while and which seemed to echo from the dark alcove as they approached.

"The extraplanar warble of the High Priest's oblations," Phillips commented. "We disturb him in his devotions."

They walked into the darkness of the alcove and as their eyes adjusted, they saw a figure upon a dais, enthroned in a magnificent and hideous shrine of gold, and masked, gloved and robed in yellow silk. It set aside a curious, boney flute, and flowed down from the dais. Phillips had been right, the way the High Priest moved bothered Holyoak. There was something wrong about it. And he couldn't seem to focus on him either.

"I have brought these ones from the Outer World," Phillips said, his voice again deep and regal.

"You prepare to leave us then." The High Priest's voice did not seem to come from a specific place, certainly not from where he was standing.

"That had been the plan," Phillips began, losing the nobility in his speech and clearing his throat. "I fear however, that they have been followed here by enemies of the Monastery."

The High Priest bowed his head at an impossible angle. It looked like resignation. "This is no fight of yours."

"No." He cleared his throat again, and looked at Holyoak and B. "But there is no other road from Leng but the one your enemies stand on."

Holyoak looked at B. "I'm tired of running from this fight anyway, Xavier," she told him, steeling her jaw.

"And you, holy man?" the High Priest looked at Holyoak, who looked away. The High Priest's gaze made his skin prickle like electricity. "Will your god stand with mine?"

"I believe in the One God." Holyoak said.

"And all others are false?" the High Priest asked, testingly.

"Or are His aspects," Holyoak finished. It was a Silver Sabremen's tenet, and though he wasn't convinced, he felt like it would land. It did, the High Priest bending his head again at an odd angle that this time looked like agreement.

"Come," he said, gliding out in front of them with a gait that was wide and rolling. "We have much to plan before the sun sets again and our enemies walk our halls."

In the great hall by the main entrance they sat, mulling over battle plans while monks ran to and fro executing the high priest's orders. Holyoak smashed out the butt of another cigarette into a receptacle that he had some time ago realized was the top of a humanoid skull. The thought barely registered as he lit another one. Seeing B. look hungrily at it, he offered the mostly empty pack to her. She'd exhausted her own supply and took two. Out of politeness he offered one to Phillips.

"No," he said. "I need my faculties undulled."

"Well," Holyoak said, raising the cigarette from his lips, "these keep mine sharp." He did not offer one to the High Priest, who sat further down the table, occasionally commenting but usually merely sending a follower to carry out whatever part of the plan had just been discussed.

A monk in a blood-spattered apron approached with a tray of food. Holyoak watched it brought in and something about it unnerved him.

"Eat," the High Priest said, almost a command.

Phillips raised a hand. "My friends are not accustomed to your ways, Indescribable One." He lowered his voice to Holyoak. "Best to avoid any repast while here. They eat their dead." B. blanched. Holyoak must have also because Phillips continued: "It hurts no one, and is hardly more or less hideous in concept than your sect's sacraments. I had thought that you Sabremen prided yourselves on your open minds."

"I'm not a Sabreman, just a friend."

"So the Sabremen send a mere associate and his imposing lady friend. Good of them to take my claims seriously."

"I can take care of myself," Holyoak said. "And as for B., you're looking at the only opponent the great El Sereno ever lost to in the ring."

"He'd have whupped me if he weren't such a gentleman," B. interjected. "But it's true nonetheless."

Before the conversation could continue, they heard the low, gritty rumble of souped-up motors.

"It seems to lack gravity at the moment," Phillips said dryly, "as the Clipper's gang is already upon us."

The growl of the motors rose in pitch before dying down and being replaced by the howls and hollers of the Clipper's underlings. They heard the rattle of chains, the revving of a monstrous engine, and a horrific clatter as the titanic outer gate snapped. The High Priest slinked back into the halls beyond, his monks in tow. Phillips followed him too as a heavy slamming rattled the doors. B. shook the dripping candle from the candlestick before her and used it to sweep the table clear, grinning like a she-devil as she balanced the weight and feel of it. Holyoak took her by the arm and led her the way that the others had gone. He stood in the archway, watching as the door splintered beneath the weight of a broken and wheelless hotrod. The car had been fused together and mounted with a chunky, pointed fender that gleamed in the torchlight as it splintered through. Four great inhuman brutes in leather jackets held it by its enlarged door handles, wielding it as a battering ram. Holyoak watched long enough to see a row of monks appear in the arches above the hall and let a volley of flaming arrows into the crowd of monsters that swelled through the doorway and over the now limp chrome and metal ram.

Holyoak followed the way his friends had gone, past goatish monks bleating horribly as they ran by him into the fray. He glimpsed the monstrous horde run through the corridors and ramparts near him, and the monks running headlong into the teeth of their attack. They had spent the day in planning, but ultimately he saw that the monks' only objective was to protect the Indescribable One. Holyoak entered a passage into the sanctuary, which was already being overrun from all sides. Backed against the ring of altars stood the High Priest and Phillips. B. stood between them and a trio of deformed creatures. Her leg muscles rippled beneath the swirl of her dress as she swung her candlestick, knocking each back in turn only to have him regroup and come at her again. Holyoak stopped for a moment in the hallway, his hands clasped, his concentration drowning out the sounds of battle. He gave himself over to his God in silent prayer. Whether it was Holy Spirit or just the spike of adrenaline that filled him in moments like these he never asked. He felt *something* fill him, move through him. He felt the overwhelming pride he had confessed to B. rise up, and he gave that to God too. He marched into the sanctuary, pulling two Colt 45s from the shoulder holsters beneath his jacket on either side.

"Break their teeth, O God, in their mouth!" he shouted as he entered the open space. A pair of snake-faced, fanged hooligans lurched at him, their tongues hanging from their mouths, and he dispatched them one after the other with a single shot from each gun. "Break out the great teeth of the young lions, O Lord!" he continued, moving past them without stopping as they fell. From a nearby corridor, a thing that was all gangly limbs leapt out at him, but a shot square in its middle sent it squealing back into the darkness it had shambled from. Holyoak took up a position near B., his back to Phillips and the High Priest. He unloaded his guns into the snarling crowd, clearing all but the foes B. faced, which were now down to two, their partner lying with a cracked skull and with his teeth biting the stone floor. Unhesitatingly, he reloaded the guns from his pocket in a series of smooth movements. "The righteous shall rejoice when he seeth the vengeance," he continued, almost to himself. A nauseous crunch to his side signaled the fall of the second of B.'s foes, who fell to the ground, his jaw crooked on his face. A scaly-faced creature with a pack of cigarettes in his t-shirt sleeve and a jagged switchblade emerged suddenly from another corridor. Holyoak fired and the creature jibbered and shuddered uncontrollably, blood spurting between its fingers as it clutched its throat. "He shall wash his feet in the blood of the wicked!" Holyoak proclaimed.

"Damn you to hell!" B. shouted, calling his attention back. Her last opponent was a head taller even than her, with a chained leather jacket and a flattop that only emphasized the ugliness of his square, tusked face. They were locked in a wrestle and B. was losing ground. "Damn you straight to hell!" she repeated, from between gritted teeth.

"Amen!" Holyoak shouted, leveling the gun in his right hand. The hammer clicked, the barrel roared, and the side of the thug's head turned to pulp as it fell away.

"Reverend Holyoak!" Phillips shouted, barely dislodging himself from the High Priest's grasp as the Indescribable One plunged silkily over the altars and disappeared into the great black well. "He nearly took me with him!" Phillips said, stunned. A silence had fallen over the sanctuary, the smell of blood and gunpowder hanging in the air like incense.

A sinister chuckle reverberated in air, and the Clipper entered, wearing a blue suit now, and this time it was sharp and well pressed. Bugba and his team huddled behind him, bruised and bloody but still wearing their bowling shirts. "That's them boss!" shouted Runt from behind his wolfish leader. The Clipper's single eye widened as it took in the sights of carnage.

"You two have cost me a lot of good soldiers," he said snidely. "Still I should thank you for getting me here." He snapped his clawed fingers. "Get the book boys." Bugba and his friends moved towards the weird shrine where the book sat, now undefended, its great blind guards sprawled dead on the floor surrounded by the enemies they had taken with them. B. brandished her dented and bloody candlestick. Holyoak leveled his pistols. Suddenly, they were both caught from behind by unseen attackers. Bugba and his little gang joined in, striking wildly and hard. Holyoak freed himself from the grip of his sneaking enemy and turned round, firing two shots into the belly of a gorilla-faced greaser.

"Where's Phillips?" he asked frantically. Before B. could answer he saw him, sneaking his way to the book, tiptoeing over the corpses to take it from its resting place. Phillips and Holyoak locked eyes for a moment as the earth began to shake violently. Phillips turned and ran with the book down a darkened passage.

"B!" Holyoak shouted, "Let's get out of here!" Taking advantage of the chunks of falling stone crashing all around them with each titanic tremor, the pair ran into the dark passage after Phillips and quickly overtook him.

"That book better be worth it," B. said, and grabbed his arm to drag him along.

They heard the Clipper's wolf cry, even over the grinding of the earth. They stopped in an open chamber, corridors running off at odd angles all around them. "Which way?" Holyoak demanded, his face inches from Phillips'. The old man was gasping for air, but indicated a passage to the right. "Are you sure?" he demanded, his sense of direction confused by the seemingly inconsistent dimensions of the monastery. The Clipper's howl sounded again, closer.

"No time, Xavier!" B. shouted, dragging Phillips with her into the passage. A blue-skinned, sharp-toothed creature burst into the chamber behind them, and Holyoak shot it in the middle of its three eyes before following. The passage was totally dark, and he followed the sound of B.'s heels on the stones. At last it opened into the great hall where the attack had started. Goatish monks in bloody yellow robes lay everywhere, torn and broken like dolls, their bodies mixed indiscriminately with those of the Clipper's deformed bikers, greasers, and thugs. Navigating the carnage, they climbed over the still shining battering ram car and found themselves outside in inky night, the light of alien stars reflecting on the row upon row of the Clipper Gang's twisted, customized cars. Many were running, with horrific occupants yelling and shouting and breaking bottles of foul-colored liquor. Others climbed about on the wreckage of the gate as it lay crooked on the ground, chained to a semi as tall as an apartment block. One car, dropped and stretched to absurdity and with human skulls along its front fender, made a shrieking dash towards them as they blindly ran to where they hoped the Bel Air was still parked.

Holyoak thanked God sincerely in his heart that the car was still there, though he found it surrounded by more ugly hooligans who were pulling at the trim. He fired, dispatching the stunned vandals and taking his driver's side mirror back from a dead hand as he stepped over them to enter the car. He admitted to himself that his rage was only partly righteous, the rest that of a man whose ride has been messed with.

B. unceremoniously shoved Phillips into the back seat before climbing over to sit next to Holyoak as he started the car. "How're we getting out of here, Xavier?" she asked, watching as the cars sped up towards them from all around.

"Not the way we came," Holyoak said coolly. He looked at Phillips in the rear-view mirror. "That road wouldn't take us back anyway, would it?"

"No," Phillips admitted. He held up the gnarled and ancient book. "But this will, if you can gain enough time for me to use it."

Holyoak shifted the car into gear and sped off around the side of the monastery, the tires screaming. "Better get started then."

Phillips began to chant from the book in a low voice as Holyoak veered back and forth, dodging the wildly put-together cars that hurtled towards them. At last he turned the car towards the open side of the plateau, into the dark. The Clipper suddenly stood in the headlights, brandishing his claws. Holyoak slammed the gas pedal, and the car bobbed first in the front and then in the back as it ran him down.

"Got him!" B. hollered. Holyoak didn't have the heart to tell her that he saw the Clipper get up and dust himself off in the rear-view mirror as they sped away. He'd settle with him another day.

Phillips continued to chant, his voice rising and becoming grand and somber again. They became aware of a sound, like distant chimes becoming louder, but as though they came from a world away. B. suddenly realized which direction they were going.

"Xavier, what are you doing!?" she shouted frantically, clutching her seat.

"Do you trust me, B.?" he asked, calmly.

"I trust you Xavier," she said, calm herself now.

He hoped she didn't see him glance back at Phillips, who nodded slowly to him without taking his eyes off the book as his chanting continued. Almost at that moment, the ground gave way beneath them and they plunged into the chasm around the monastery. The headlights glanced upon gruesome shapes along the craggy walls that instantly retreated from them and then shone straight down into a darkness they did not reflect back from. Phillips' chanting rose to a high volume as he intoned: "IA! IA!"

The car bounced deeply on its suspension as it landed squarely on its smoking tires. The light of day was sudden and stung their eyes as the smoke parted and they found themselves parked on a lonely stretch of road in Arizona. A signpost marked SR 16 marked a turn-off just before them for a moment, before both the sign and the road it pointed to faded away, leaving them on a charred patch of blacktop, only the book in Phillips' lap and the old man himself to show where they had been.

The Valley and the Shadow

Prologue

THE WRESTLER stood firm on the patch of dry, desert earth. His body was bronze and toned, and his golden mask glinted in the lowering sunlight.

Across from him stood the quarry that he had been seeking. It was a figure of a man, but low and squatting, too wide and thick to look right to his eyes. It was wrapped in a heavy coat despite the heat. The coat was of a practical cut but a rich and luxurious fabric. It was old, but had aged without undue wear. It could have been made for a pirate, a naval officer, or a wealthy landowner and not looked out of place. Even now, it would not have stood out in a crowd except for its unassuming opulence.

The face of the being that wore that coat was old too. Gnarled and coarse, the features as wide and squat as the body. A huge mouth grinned with thick and sharp teeth in his direction.

"So, Serene One," he said flatly. His voice was clear, but it seemed a labor to get the words through his toothy maw. "You have found me. Now what shall you do with me?"

There were foes the wrestler had fought who deserved speeches. This was the truest monster he had ever faced. He knew that this thing was responsible for untold death around the world and for millennia.

He grunted, propelling himself towards his foe's heavy shape. The creature did not move, did not flinch. He launched into its torso with all of his strength and did not budge the thing. He felt the creature's ribs, like the great planks of a ship as he held him in his vice-like grip—and he felt him laugh, low and silent and first, then shaking with glee.

Suddenly, the monster struck back. The wrestler was surprised that he was able to keep his hold, but the blow rattled his bones, and disturbed his sacred connection to the rhythms of the Earth. He feinted left and jerked his body right, but his foe was too low and too heavy to be pulled down. He focused, searching out the powers of the animals in the desert around him: the quickness of the lizard, the coiled strength of the rattlesnake. He shouted again, butting his head against his opponent's. He saw stars, the monster's head being even harder than it looked, but he had managed to daze it, to shake its impenetrable balance. Now he could take the offensive.

He struck at the creature with clasped hands. His blows were blocked and the arms they fell upon were like iron, but the blows landed like hammers and he slowly lost ground. At last the wrestler saw a better opening and seized him from behind under the arm and under the neck in an unbreakable hold. The thing flailed and moaned and raged, the wrestler was like a ragdoll on his back but did not let go.

Enraged, the monster screamed, ducking low and leaping into the air in a flourish of smoke. He sprouted wings, a beak, and a long horny crest, and the wrestler found his hands wrapped in the matted furry tufts of something like a shaggy pterodactyl. The creature continued to rise, its wings flapping open as it soared upwards.

The sun was low but still visible above the horizon. He had never seen a vampire that change shape in the sunlight before. This was something new.

The wrestler held on for his life, his vision going dark as they rose higher and higher towards the thin whisps of cloud in the arid sky. Then with a horrible shriek, the monstrous, leathery bird turned over, the sky and the earth changed places, and the luchador's vision began to shift into a deep and blinding red. He dug his hands in more deeply, unable to see the enemy that desperately tried to buck him into the open sky. He cleared his mind, filling it with an ancient Aztec chant and stilled his body, relaxing his spirit though his limbs held like a tightened spring and the desert wind sang high in his ears as they plummeted again the Earth below.

I

XAVIER HOLYOAK woke up with contentment in his heart. This had been something rare once, but in the three months he had spent in this Oklahoma town it had become familiar. He had come to this town on a plea for help against what turned out to be a pretty standard haunting. The ghost had been a bad sort of man in life, but was easy to lay once his petty reasons for sticking around had been figured out. It was an accident that he had met Dawn if such a thing as an accident existed in his life. She had invited him into her life and into her home. It was in her bed that he lay, and her breath was sweet and low as she sighed, turning in the sheets next to him, letting a slender hand play on his bare chest and abdomen.

She caressed his scars as she often did—the burned and half-healed flesh, the jagged bullet holes and the purple lines left by broken bones. She never asked about any of them, never commented at all, merely loved them for being part of him, and now her passions rose as she stoked his own, her love as innocent and wild as Eve in the garden.

Holyoak couldn't fathom that his God would have any objection to her. On a good day, he could even believe that she was a gift from Him. At any rate, in those three months the horrible burden on his conscience that would have compelled him to move on had not appeared.

On a better day, he could let himself believe that she was the sign sent to tell him his work was finally done.

After they rose and began the day, Holyoak slipped on his worn boots and put on his bomber jacket. He was still cautious, still ready, still wearing the huge Colts underneath it. And he put his cleric's collar on too.

It was Friday, and that meant a drive into town for supplies. He stopped at post office in town first, anxiety nibbling around his heart as it did every week. Relief and shame mixed when the mail proved inconsequential—no important news and no long letters describing supernatural woes and asking for help.

It was coming out of the post office that he saw her.

"Jezebel," he said the name like it was a curse. He'd met this creature before, in unfavorable circumstances. She was dressed like some biker's girlfriend, in a short leopard-skin skirt with tall, high-heeled boots and a scarf tied between her chin and the heaving bosom in a half-buttoned shirt two sizes too small. She had a streak of blond died into her jet-black bangs and the sharp little nub of a horn was just visible underneath that side. Just as he had noticed when they first met, her feet were very large and weren't shaped quite right in a way that made him happy they were hidden by her boots. Otherwise her body was something—and anything but heavenly.

She was smoking, and exhaled a long plume of blue in his direction. Holyoak impatiently fanned his hand in front of his face, scattering the smoke.

"Hiya, Reverend," she said, like a cat particularly pleased with its ability to catch mice.

"What do want," he asked between gritted team, taking her roughly by the arm.

"Hey," she pouted, "that's no way to treat a lady,"

"And you're no lady."

She shrugged. "Well, you got me there." She pulled an envelope from her pocket and waved it in his face. "Special delivery."

Holyoak snatched it away. "What is this?"

"I don't know," Jezebel smirked, twirling a strand of hair between her fingers, moving dangerously close as she let the cigarette dangle in one corner of her mouth. "But it must be important. Somebody's gone to a lot of trouble to keep it from getting delivered. Just ask all those dead mailmen."

Holyoak looked down at the letter. It was yellowed and crumpled, with no return address and only his name written in pen. It was also flecked with dried blood.

"And what do you care about this?" he asked.

"Oh, you did me a good turn once," she said, before turning on the most devilish of pouts. "And it's no fun being a bad girl if you can't make your dear old dad angry once in a while—even if it means being good."

Holyoak kept the letter in his pocket until he got home to Dawn's house. It was a tiny house that had been her grandmother's and still had much of an antiquated domesticity to it. He went to the bookcase on the far end of the room. This part of the house was all Dawn's. A pink portable record player sat on one shelf surrounded by ballerina figures and a hodgepodge of vinyl 45s scattered in and out of their boxes. A Hank Williams single sat still on it with the needle halfway through the track. He smiled ruefully as he turned it on. He hated when she left a record stopped like that, but it was something that would always make him think of her. With a warping sound as the player came up to speed, Hank started singing about cheating hearts, and Holyoak felt accused. He took the letter out of his jacket and stared at its red-dotted envelope as he turned it in his fingers.

The door opened, and he turned to see Dawn. She held a paper bag of groceries, and she had dressed like a queen to go shopping. Black flats, nylons, a tight blue dress with a round buckled belt at her waist. Her blonde hair was kept by a little blue hat pinned in place. "Hey baby," she said, her voice thick with the country. "I'm making your favorite, spaghetti."

Holyoak smiled sadly. Spaghetti wasn't his favorite. She was. He felt like a naughty child who would have to come clean about some wrong.

"What's wrong, baby?" she asked, shifting the groceries in her arms as she went to him so she could stroke his weather-beaten face.

Wordlessly, he handed her the letter. She froze. She knew just enough of his life from the circumstances that had brought him here. Like him, she had known somewhere deep that this day could come.

"Have you read it yet."

"No," he whispered. Shaking his head. "I don't have to." He knew that was a lie as soon as he said it. The familiar call on his heart was starting to set in.

"Yes, you do," she said her voice flat and firm. She had set the groceries on the table and leaned on it desperately, but she looked at him fiercely now.

"I know," he sighed.

"Will you come back?" She looked even more intently at him. "To me?"

"Yes," he lied. And it made him feel worse. He broke her gaze when he said it. "Of course."

"Well, you're going to need a full stomach aren't you."

He had expected anger or at least coldness. But she was her smiling self by the time dinner was on the table. She loved him long and sweetly into the night, abandoning herself wholly to her passions. He held her until morning, unsleeping, trying to memorize every detail of her face and the way that her body felt pressed against his.

In the morning Holyoak rose early, kissing her forehead as she slept and sneaking out of the house into the cold morning. He sat in the Bel Air trying to find the strength to do something until he realized he had better leave before she woke up and he had to say goodbye and make more promises that God might not let him keep.

"How long, Lord?" he asked aloud. He struck the steering wheel with his fist. "How long?!"

He stewed, wanting to resist, wanting to disobey, his heart begging for a sign. But there was only the nagging feeling in his chest, the commandment to move on.

"Will you ever be done with me, Lord?" he asked bitterly of the clear blue sky. "Give me a sign." The call in his heart was so strong now he could almost hear the command: "Go."

He stopped a little before the highway to open the letter. He set his jaw as he read it, then stuffed the open letter roughly into his pocket, taking the highway south, towards Texas.

II

AS WAS usual on these trips, Holyoak fumbled with the radio as he drove. It was the middle of a sticky summer, and the sun was bright in his eyes, even when it was high in the sky above the Bel Air. It had been some time since he had seen another vehicle, and the last few he had crossed paths with had been freight trucks. The road was particularly straight here, and the radio had nothing to pick up in the wide-open space. Absentmindedly, he turned the dial now and then, catching bits of barely recognizable tunes beneath the static.

He would turn it off completely if he couldn't find a station that was playing something. Eventually. Until then it was an exercise in hope.

The static rose, warbling, and a voice he hadn't heard in quite some time broke through:

"…right boys and ghouls, they say our friend Holyoak is on the move again…" The clarity of the signal rose and fell. Holyoak scowled at the radio. Then a sign caught his attention as the static built again. It was shaped like twin tablets and said "THOU SHALT HAVE NO OTHER GODS BEFORE ME"

"Well," the voice emerged again, "keep listening to your friend, the Kustom Kreeper, and we'll give you some helpful—" A second sign was visible on the side of the road: "THOU SHALT NOT MAKE ANY GRAVEN THING"

His knuckles gripped the wheel until they were white.

"Are you out there listening, Holyoak?" the voice on the radio continued.

THOU SHALT NOT TAKE THE LORD'S NAME IN VAIN

"We know where you're heading and—"

KEEP THE SABBATH HOLY

"—you'd turn back if you knew—"

HONOR THY FATHER AND MOTHER

"But then again, hee hee, maybe you wouldn't…"

THOU SHALT NOT MURDER

"—okay to break the rules if your boss tells you—"

THOU SHALT NOT ADULTURIZE

"Hee hee hee…"

THOU SHALT NOT STEAL

"We'll have to see, friends, if God's own holy hitman can face the music when the chips are down and the way isn't clear…"

THOU SHALT NOT BEAR FALSE WITNESS

"The Old Master says 'I'll be seeing you soon', and with an invitation like that, who could resist—"

THOU SHALT NOT COVET

As he passed the last of the signs, the radio cut into music for a song or two—wild, psychotic country songs of murder and rape that he listened to intently and in vain for some kind of clue before the static again overwhelmed whatever hellish station this was intruding into his car.

When the signal was gone, he angrily turned the radio off.

It was an old, Spanish-style mission that the directions in the letter brought him too. There hadn't been much info, just directions and a prayer to come "for the sake of the children."

Holyoak stopped the Bel Air near the gate. It was kicking up dust from the dirt road, and a thick layer of loose grime had dulled its usually black sheen. He got out of the car, gently closing the door and standing with his hand on his hips, holding his jacket open so that his white collar would be visible to the monks that lingered nearby doing chores. It would help in this case to be one of them, more or less.

"*Puedo ayudarse, padre*?" one of the monks asked, and receiving no answer but a blank stare repeated again in English: "May I help you, father?"

"No father for me, sir." Holyoak said. Just reverend. Rev. Xavier Holyoak.

"I'm expected."

Holyoak was whisked through the gate and into the cool interior of the mission church. There seemed to be a great deal of excitement over his appearance. He was brought before a young man who was scrubbing the church floor with a coarse brush and a simple wooden bucket. The young man wore the plain brown habit and tonsured hair of the other monks, and was clean-shaven, though he barely looked like he needed to shave. He rose to his sandaled feet as Holyoak approached.

"You are the Rev. Holyoak?" the monk asked.

"Yes. I'm expected."

"You are very late," a new voice interjected. It came from a great mountain of a man in a blue, pinstriped, three-piece suit. His hands and the area around his eyes and mouth were the bronze of a statue, but most of his face was covered in golden mask.

Holyoak recognized him, of course. Sereno, the most famous wrestler in the world, and a movie star to boot. It seemed the rumors of his off-stage exploits were at least partly true.

"Reverend," the monk said reassuringly. "We wrote to you several months ago."

"I know," Holyoak groaned. "There were some problems getting your message through the mail. What seems to be the trouble."

The monk gestured for him to walk with him and the others who had brought him went along, as well as Sereno. "We are not far from the border," he said. "Increasingly, there had been reports of something, something ancient and evil." The monk hesitated.

"You understand that many people come north into this country in search of work and a better life for their families?"

"I'm familiar with the situation, yes." Holyoak was feeling slightly impatient. He had driven a long way and he had been gearing up for a fight. Somebody needed to point him in the right direction—and soon.

"Sometimes they stop here on the way. The mission, you understand, offers protection to anyone who seeks it. Everyone is welcome here."

"I understand," Holyoak was getting frustrated. "Your letter spoke of something evil that was hunting people—children. It was made to sound urgent, so I came as soon as I was made aware. Look, maybe you'd better take me to your abbot or superior or—"

One of the monks attending giggled. The other, a fat but muscular man spoke up. "Brother Francisco is the abbot, *señor*."

Holyoak must have looked incredulous at this, because the young abbot took a moment to compose himself before continuing. "Thank you, Brother Rodrigo. We began to hear stories of people, and children as you say, disappearing on the journey through the desert. Stories of something that stalked and hunted whole travelling parties. Then people began to appear with scars." The abbot gestured towards his neck.

"A vampire?" Holyoak asked. Experience had taught him to hate vampires most of all.

"Not like any I have ever seen," Sereno interjected. "Older probably, immensely powerful—and profoundly… different from any I have ever faced."

The abbot continued. "I made the mistake of asking my bishop for help. He dismissed it as the superstitions of ignorant peasants. I intended to reach out to the Silver Sabremen, but the bishop learned of it, and strictly forbade me involving that forbidden club."

"So you reached out to me."

The abbot bowed his head. "We know that you have worked with the Sabremen, knew of your reputation." They had reached a very old door of wood and iron.

"And you neglected to tell the bishop."

The abbot bowed again, smiling.

"Looks like you hedged your bets though." Holyoak craned his neck towards Sereno.

"It seemed prudent when we hadn't heard back from you to look elsewhere."

Holyoak actually had great respect for Sereno. Knew of him and his work, knew the Sabremen trusted him. But he didn't like the idea of playing second fiddle. It rankled him, and then his conscience convicted him of pride.

"Well," Holyoak began, trying to set that pride aside for the greater good. "Where do we start? What do we know?"

The monks looked at each other, but the abbot looked at Sereno, who stood with his arms crossed in front of him, then back at Holyoak.

"I'm afraid you misunderstand. Sereno has already captured the creature. It is here," he said, indicating the heavy door before them, "in the church's basement."

III

USUALLY, ON those rare occasions when a vampire was captured rather than killed, a delicate chain of silver draped around its body was enough to hold the creature immobile. But the monstrous thing at the end of this vast, brazier-lit space was held in bonds of thick, massive chain, still glistening silver but much more than solid than a symbol.

At first, Holyoak thought the vampire was squatting. He was dressed in the sort of timelessly antiquated way that he was accustomed to seeing immortal creatures sport but he was clearly not based on a proper human mold. His body was wide, thick and solid, his hands huge and rough, his brow hairy and sloping—clearly, a Neanderthal.

Though clearly not like any he had seen or heard of. Its mouth was nearly forced open by the uneven rows broad, pointed teeth, it's eyes like the slits of a snake or a great cat. Clearly, the Curse reacted differently on a being like this had been—human perhaps, but no son of Adam.

As they approached, Holyoak realized that they were in a dungeon. Racks, wheels, and iron cages littered the great, dim room. Holyoak realized that Brother Francisco and his monks weren't leading them in a straight line from the door, instead veering towards the wall at the right. Holyoak looked around, suddenly aware of something dangerous behind them—it was the torturer's pendulum, its semicircular blade replaced by a ten-foot-long tree trunk, sawed down to the finest point it would hold. The mechanism was held up above the door, a simple control panel of knobs not far from where the creature was imprisoned. Holyoak saw that it was rigged so that if the vampire made the slightest move beyond where the chains held him fast, it would come swinging down with a tremendous, coiled force, driving the foot-wide stake through the monster's chest.

The vampire merely stared at the floor beneath hooded lids, unmoving and unblinking as they approached.

"Speak," said a voice, low and surprisingly elegant despite sounding like it came from someone with a mouth full of rocks. "Or leave me."

Holyoak had seen evils, ancient and new. He felt a deep emptiness in this monster's presence—a sadness even. He did not realize that he spoke aloud:

"I was dumb with silence, I held my peace, even from good, and my sorrow was stirred."

The creature raised its head slightly, eyes still downcast. "Old King David's song sounds strange, bent to this soft and flouncy tongue. Could it be?"

He looked up. Something like interest lighting his lined and hairy face. His eyes glinted like yellow topaz and his gaze fixed Holyoak where he stood. He twisted his misshapen mouth into something resembling a smile, his thick, bluntly pointed teeth protruding like twisted spikes.

"First the Serene One, and now the one they call God's Hitman." He stared now at Brother Francisco, who stood upright and tried resolutely to look unafraid. "Truly, Abbot, you have spared no expense in welcoming me."

"Why haven't you destroyed this—" Holyoak's voice was dry, his face bent with disgust "—thing."

God's command was clear in his heart. Holyoak produced a fine, laurel stake from his jacket and moved towards the bound horror, too quickly for the young abbot or his helpers to hold him back, he closed the distance fast—a wide stride in heavy, loud boots. With skill he brought the point of the stake towards where he hoped the creature's heart was in its misshapen body.

It snapped like a twig against its ribs.

The monks seized him, pulling him away.

"He has demanded sanctuary!" Brother Francisco shouted.

"Sanctuary!" Holyoak nearly choked on the word in shock. "You granted it sanctuary?" He gestured wildly at the apparatuses of woe around them. "And now what, you'll throw your own little inquisition for him?"

"We are not proud of the church's legacy here," Brother Francisco said, leading him gently away. "The excesses of the Mexican Inquisition are rivalled only by its mother in Spain. I often reflect on how many innocent Christians were killed in this very place because of their convictions."

"And how many Aztecs?" Sereno spoke up, deep in thought as though disturbed to be there.

A low laugh came from where the chained monster stood. "A pity your God has such fools for followers."

They all looked back askance, none of them willing to engage that obvious bait with a response.

Holyoak shook off the arms of the monks that still led him back toward the exit and continued toward it himself.

"Maybe," he said his eyebrows raised and his jaw tight, glaring at the young abbot eye to eye. "And how many sorcerers?"

A few days had passed, and Holyoak had more or less worked his way into a routine with the monks, helping with some of the daily chores and keeping to his book of psalms in the company of their daily prayers.

Sereno kept mainly to himself and his meditations in the cell that they had given him, but Holyoak recognized the kindred spirit of another hunter in the taut energy with which he carried himself in communal spaces.

This morning, Holyoak found himself in the kitchen with Brother Francisco, peeling a seemingly endless supply of potatoes for the bland evening stew that the monks would share at the end of the day.

"The community will eat well tonight," the abbot said, with exaggerated admiration of Holyoak's skill with a knife.

"And what about your other guest? What's he eating these days?" Holyoak rankled at the thought of the thing that lay beneath them in the dungeon below.

"We have offered him lamb's blood, but he has refused." Brother Francisco stiffened and avoided his gaze. Similar conversations had been had before.

"He's old," Holyoak said dryly. "As old as Adam if there's any truth to the stories you say he's been telling. A vampire that old doesn't need to feed often." Holyoak laughed bitterly. "But when he does…" he whistled. "It'll be an ocean of blood that he can put away."

"Brother Xavier," the young abbot said, drawing his breath. "I am aware that you do not approve of keeping this creature alive. There are protocols in place to—"

Holyoak sighed. The monk might understand him—might even sympathize with his feeling that every moment he left that creature in its dim semblance of life was a spit at God's grace. But he was talking to a Catholic, with a set way of doing things in mind. He had bucked the rules, but would only go so far.

"When does the bishop's investigator get here?" Holyoak asked.

"Tomorrow."

"And you don't think," Holyoak grinned ironically, "that he's going to have something to say about you taking matters into your own hands this far?"

"Probably. But when he tells the bishop what he has seen," Francisco held his paring knife up in triumph, "what else can the bishop do but admit that he was wrong?"

An old, stooped brother approached and whispered in the abbot's ear, whose face lit up.

"Speak of the Devil and his advocate," Francisco said, smiling. "The bishop's aid is here."

They walked outside and across the courtyard from the mess to the monastery gate. Holyoak admired the view of the mountains that surrounded them, both far away and seemingly so close to the community's walls.

Francisco unlocked the door, and turned around, dumbfounded as the monk how had given him the news, who merely scuttled away with an embarrassed bow.

"Please come in," he said, pulling open the heavy, wooden door.

Holyoak felt his jaw drop and hoped it hadn't fallen as far as it felt. In the doorway stood a woman, in the black habit, coif, and white wimple of a nun, somehow incapable of hiding the lush charms of her body in their shapelessness. The get up was completely convincing if not for the heavy makeup and for something like high heels and a hint of fishnet stocking peeking from the ankles of her oddly shaped feet.

"Sister Jezebel," Holyoak said with obvious irony, and she flashed a fiery glare at him.

"You know each other then?" Brother Francisco asked.

"We've crossed paths once or twice." Holyoak demurred. "You meet all sorts in my line."

"An unusual name for a religious…" Francisco mused aloud.

"I've had an unusual life," Jezebel said, shaking it off with a smile. "Shall we get started?"

Down in the chamber beneath the church, even Holyoak was amazed as Jezebel's lack of fear. He realized his own hesitancy to approach the creature as they walked towards hit and his pace slowed, finally stopping as she sped on.

The monster snarled at her when she came close, but she merely took the opportunity to lift his hairy lip further and examine his horrible, drool-laden, teeth. She laid her head against his chest.

"As expected, no heartbeat."

The deep, still chest expanded, the creature taking in air to speak. "Do you mock me, halfling?"

Jezebel smiled, with what look like sweetness as she stepped back.

"As expected?" the abbot asked, unsure of where to even begin. "So the bishop believes me?"

"It doesn't matter, padre-o. I believe you. Let's get outta here." She turned back, her hips swaying rhythmically under her tight black habit, eyeing the shaggy brute over her shoulder. "I don't like the smell in here."

Back in Francisco's office, the young abbot poured them each a glass of brandy. He was visibly stunned when the ostensible nun before him downed her glass in a draft, and taking the brandy from him gently, began to drink directly from the decanter.

Holyoak smiled. He had decided to play along for the time being. He wanted to see where this was going.

"There's only one thing for it," she said, knocking back another belt. "You've got to kill it."

Both Holyoak and Francisco were surprised by this statement. Holyoak obviously knew who was making it and was curious why a monster—even a beautiful one—would advocate the destruction of another. But he was more intrigued by the abbot's response.

"Sister," he said gravely, "there is more that has come to light from this situation. I believe we should study this creature, interview him—interrogate him if you prefer."

"I'm listening," Jezebel said, arms akimbo at her supple hips.

"He is evil yes, and dangerous, but I have spoken to him on many occasions since he has been here. Despite appearances, he is not a mindless monster but an intelligent being—one that witnessed with his own eyes the Fire of Rome, the construction of the Pyramids—even our Lord's Sermon on the Mount."

"Abbot," Jezebel said, her face and voice becoming stern in a way the Holyoak couldn't help but find appealing. "You requested the bishop's involvement. You hired not one, but two shadow hunters on your own authority. You asked for help killing a monster. And now you tell me that you want to keep it as what, a pet?"

"Forgive me, sister," Francisco said, lowering his eyes. "No, I do not believe that the creature should be spared by us. Merely that we give him the opportunity for his soul to be spared by God."

Any further theological debate would have to wait. There was a knock on the door, just before it was abruptly opened. Sereno stood in the doorway, sweat visible at the patches of skin left bare by the golden mask around his eyes and mouth and at the open neck and chest of the pale blue shirt he wore.

"*Abate*," he said. "I must speak to you."

Francisco stepped aside, motioning for the wrestler to sit.

"I had felt disturbances in the Earth's vibrations, so in my meditations," he began, shaking his head as if to ground himself in his surroundings. "I touched the mind of a golden eagle. There is a great evil coming, in the hundreds, maybe the thousands."

"What, my son?" Francisco asked, placing a hand reassuringly on Sereno's great shoulder.

"Vampires, *abate*. I saw their huge, mass graves—a trail of them growing closer, merging larger from different directions."

Sereno breathed deeply, shaking the last of the vision from his eyes. "At the rate they are moving, I believe they will be here by nightfall tomorrow."

IV

HOLYOAK COULDN'T sleep that night. The monks had not placed any restrictions on his movements around the compound, but he nonetheless made his way clandestinely to the church, and finding it empty, down the old steps to the dungeon below.

As expected, the creature was awake. He was totally still, but his eyes were fixed on Holyoak as he entered the dim space. He suspected that the thing, old as it was, barely slept at all, but had perhaps slept for centuries just to pass the time.

His compulsion to destroy this monster was strong. But Francisco's thinking had caused him to question.

"Were you really at the Sermon on the Mount?" he asked.

"Yes."

The creature had to take in air to speak but had otherwise neither moved nor blinked.

"So you met Jesus?" Holyoak was skeptical, but curious.

"No."

They stared at each other for a moment, then took a deep, almost labored breath.

"Outcast thing that I am," the vampire continued, "I lived for a time among the lepers of Judea. "I never met your Jesus, but I heard him speak from time to time."

"How close were you at the mountain?"

The creature smiled his ugly grin.

"I'm certain he knew I was there, if that is your question. And *he* did not seek to strike me down." They stared at each other for a long moment. "I was aping a leper at the time, remember. I was close enough to tell you that your master's words did not translate well into Greek."

"And this experience had no impact on you?"

The creature stared at him. Almost quizzically.

"The young abbot up there thinks your soul can be saved." Holyoak started this sentence bitterly, but it ended almost like a question.

"I am no son of Adam. I am not made in the image of your God—merely one of the broken playthings he meant to throw on the dung heap of creation."

"But if you really heard Christ preach—"

"I have had this debate with Thomas Aquinas. I am doubtful that you—or the young *abbé* have anything to add."

Again, they stared each other down in silence.

"We're ready for your little rescue party," Holyoak wasn't sure what response he expected, but it wasn't the one he got. The creature looked defeated.

"So," he sighed, "they come at last, to destroy the abomination." He looked Holyoak up and down with a hungry eye. "But I have always been a lowly thing."

Holyoak felt himself caught in the vampire's gaze, unsure of whether it was interest or the monster's glamour. Slowly, he hooked a foot into the leg of one of the tables of torture nearby so that he would be aware of any steps he took forward.

"My people lived in a valley dotted by caves. We were not hunters by nature but sometimes by necessity, living mostly on roots and berries.

"Then one day, they came. You came. *Humans*. On the first few visits we traded with you, furs and skins, and pretty stones that were no more than baubles for our children but for which you had unquenchable greed, in exchange for your curious tools and knives sharper and shinier than any we had ever seen.

"Then you came back. You ignored our halloos and you used your knives not as tools but to cut off the hands raised in friendship.

"We knew some of the secrets of fire. Knew how to capture it and keep it alive. We knew it could be dangerous if disrespected, but it was life to us and unimaginable wealth. Can you image watching your family drown in a river of liquid gold?

"They burned down the little village that to us was the center of the world. They made sport of our mothers and daughters and sisters among the bodies of the menfolk before they cast them into the fire. And I—I ran, weeping like a child. Oh, I wasn't the only one, and we were children. But left and right behind me and before me, they were all cut down. As far as I know, I alone escaped. Perhaps it was luck, perhaps your God had plans for me after all. Big plans.

"I was found, dirty and alone by *her*. Another creature cast out of Paradise. Lilith, Mother of the Night. Perhaps she took pity on me, perhaps she thought it would be funny to make of me a pet. Perhaps she merely wanted to see if it could be done. She nursed me in the nights, feeding me on the black milk of her breasts, and I found myself sleeping and waking earlier, until I too, was a creature of darkness. Then she left me, left me with a nameless craving so deep that I would have gone mad had I not stumbled upon a field of aurochs and drained them all dry, wrestling the mighty animals to the ground with my hands and ripping out their living throats with teeth not yet so sharp.

"I wandered the Earth for a time, first north following the glaciers, then south into Mesopotamia, overcoming my revulsion for your kind to follow the birth of civilization as it spread into Egypt and Assyria. With great difficulty, I strained and stretched my throat beyond its natural capacities, and taught myself to speak in the great and alien cities that sprang against the wild, empty places.

"Wherever I went among you, I was at best ignored. But often I was chased, mistreated, and abused. Left outside in the cold and forced to feed on dogs.

"Despite the hatred in my heart, I did not yet know what I was—or understand my true place in things. The first time I fed on a human, it was out of necessity. I was blind with hunger, cornered by thugs in a filthy street. I can no longer remember when or where this was, only the look of surprised terror on the face of my victim as the life drained from his face, his last words a cry for help from friends who had already long run away.

"But I found that his blood nourished me in a way that the blood of beasts could not. It made me stronger, faster, heightened my senses. There was no going back."

"Eventually I learned that there were others like me, except that they had been human in their first lives. I sought one out in Alexandria. But I was met with a horror no less than that with which your kind greeted me.

"Decades later, in what had become Baghdad, vampire assassins sought to end my life. I overcame them easily, tossing their dried-out husks into the Tigris. This was a delicacy like none I had ever known. I knew better than to willfully hunt them, but there would be other attempts, and each time I would drain them and grow stronger, wiser, and more dangerous by taking their power.

"Have you ever wondered why vampires do not hunt each other? It is their greatest taboo. So I had learned that I was an outcast even among the monsters. The death they would bestow on a vampire who had killed another might take centuries. But I am an abomination to them as much as to you.

"I can feel the creatures coming to me in their hundreds. But they do not come to rescue me. I have been hunted to the ends of the earth, but I am crafty. Nonetheless, I have never stayed still for so long.

"I am perhaps the oldest vampire left in the world. Can you imagine what would be gained by another that drank from my blood? Can you imagine a generation in the hundreds with my power?

"So you will have to choose, shall I be destroyed to prevent greater evil, even at the cost of a soul your abbot thinks can be saved? Or shall you risk testing your God's mercy."

Holyoak realized that he had moved closer to the monster. His foot was still hooked in the table leg, but he had brought it with him several feet.

"God's mercy does not need to be tested." Holyoak said. But he did feel some doubt. How could someone have been in the presence of Jesus and not have been changed? And if he was wholly evil, then why did God's own son not cast him out. It occurred to him that he could have been lying, but he had the strangest sensation that he wasn't.

He drew a wooden stake from beneath his jacket, and approached with purpose. The creature laughed. It took Holyoak a moment to realize that his feet had stopped moving and that he was rooted to the spot.

"Perhaps I wish to give my blood freely for my people, as your Christ did for yours," the vampire sneered. "Or perhaps I wish only to take as many with me into death as possible. At any rate, do not imagine that these chains prevent me from controlling my fate."

Holyoak left quickly, a superstitious and primal chill in his bones. The night for him would be brief and shallow.

THINGS MOVED quickly the next morning out of necessity. Brother Francisco gave Sereno permission to teach the monks how to fight, and they were in the courtyard after breakfast practicing drills with simple, wooden staves.

Holyoak mentioned that they would need weapons, and he went out to the Bel Air to add the old sawed-off and blessed machete to the Colts that never left his side.

There seemed to be no shortage of underground cellars in the monastery complex, and Francisco had taken them to another hidden, underground room at daybreak.

"The treasure of Santa Anna!" he had proclaimed, whipping the heavy drapes off of a row of crumbling wooden crates and stirring more dust than hope when Holyoak and Sereno surveyed the ancient guns and ammunition.

But it was a start, and Holyoak sat now, across from Jezebel—an erstwhile ally for whatever reason of her own—carefully separating bullets from casings. They had found a good supply of guns—some old enough to have actually belonged to Santa Anna, some certainly more recent. The monks of old had clearly had no problem looking the other way for the old general or for others after him, and Holyoak reflected that in his experience with Men of God, a donation of the right size could work all manner of miracles.

"So what's your angle?" he asked after pulling a long drag off his cigarette. He had found himself looking her over in her nun outfit with a mixture of amusement and animal admiration, but there had been mostly silence between them. She had adept and nimble fingers for this kind of work and was actually surpassing him in output. "And where's the real investigator?"

"Oh, face down in some tavern." She raised a red-nailed finger coyly. "Nothing to do with me, though it does sound like my kind of idea. I just heard there was an opening for the job"

"I suppose." Holyoak squinted at her. "But I don't see any advantage to you in helping some poor little community of monks fight off a wave of vampires."

The door opened and Francisco entered. Two young brothers crouched behind the doorway for a peak. Jezebel merely looked at Holyoak and winked.

Sure, Holyoak thought, there were plenty of God-fearing men to lead astray here, and he shook his head knowingly as if accepting that answer.

"Will these do?" the abbot asked, setting down an old crate full of chalices and candlesticks.

Holyoak stood up, rummaging through the wares, some old and tarnished.

"Most of it," he said. "We need pure silver, or as pure as possible."

"I have the monks rummaging through the old stores. but we are a poor community."

"What about the cup and plate from the altar?" Holyoak said coldly.

"Those are the sacred vessels used in the Mass, reverend."

"Even better." He put a hand on the monk's shoulder. "I'm sorry, brother. We need every scrap of silver—especially if it's consecrated. It still won't be enough, but it'll have to do."

"You believe that I am responsible for this situation," the abbot asked.

"I believe you should have killed the thing when you had the chance." Holyoak took a deep breath. "But then again, I've tried. Maybe it wouldn't have made a difference."

"He is full of resentment and hurt. If only we had more time." The abbot still seemed convinced. Holyoak was beginning to think there was more happening than met the eye.

"You never read Marlowe in the seminary, did ya?" Jezebel chimed in. Francisco merely shook his head. "Trust me. In my line of work, I know. Repentance doesn't work that way."

The rest of the day, the monks frantically searched every chamber, basement, and cell. They gathered family relics, crucifixes, candelabras, and old coins. Holyoak heated the forge, and while the brothers rested or searched between combat drills, Sereno worked it, his bronze body and golden mask glistening in the heat of its flames. They had found casts for bullets in various sizes, including—much to Holyoak's delight—Long Colt, and they worked tirelessly until they had used the last drop of molten silver.

Then they set about breaking down wooden crosses, chair legs, and even the communion rail. They sharpened the ends of the monk's staves and fashioned the rest into stakes, except for the crucifixes, which were crushed down to splinters and packed with the coarse salt the monks used into Holyoak's shotgun shells.

Jezebel absented herself from these tasks for obvious reasons, not willing to risk her identity being outed by a smoking burn on the skin or an uncontrollable hiss escaping her lush, ruby lips. But she worked to set torches along the walls and throughout the courtyard with the remaining monks, and as night fell the monastery remained an oasis of light.

Holyoak stood in his waiting stance, machete at his belt, sawed-off shotgun resting over his shoulder, and one of the Colts in his right hand. Jezebel stood at his left, loading two mismatched pistols, careful not to touch the silver tips of the bullets, and Brother Francisco at his right, brandished his staff forward. The young and strong among the monks stood in a half-circle behind them, armed with sharpened staves, while the old or the skilled, took up strategic positions on the walls.

"But the walls will protect us, yes?" Francisco asked, fearing the answer. "A vampire must be invited?"

"If this was a cloister, maybe. But you said it yourself, everyone is welcome here."

There was a chilling stillness in the night beyond their walls. Holyoak craned his neck, listening and realized that it was the absence of noise that was calling his attention. No birds, no rustling rodents—not so much as a damn cricket. He knew that the enemy was close.

He saw it a split second before the bell sounded: tiny points of light, glinting red in the darkness. The robed figure in the bell tower rang again, then cast off his cowl revealing his masked face.

No longer needing to hide, Sereno pulled away a heavy drape from in front of him, revealing an old-style Gatling gun mounted just above the wall of the belfry, and fired as soon as the first vampires stepped into the light.

The vampires swelled out of the darkness, initially haughty at the spray of bullets, until they noticed their flesh sloughing away or found themselves bound to the ground by the bits of silver in their bodies.

Down in the courtyard, Holyoak and the rest stood their ground. The brothers on the walls had joined in, the loud cracks of their gunfire punctuating randomly against the steady pulses of the Gatling gun.

The monks behind him were nervous. Francisco began to pray in Latin, and the some of the brothers joined him.

Somehow, despite the difference in language, Holyoak recognized it, and joined in English, his voice soon rising above the rest, his conviction steeling those around him:

"Yea, though I walk through the valley of the shadow of death, I will fear no evil: for thou art with me; thy rod and thy staff they comfort me.

"Thou preparest a table before me in the presence of mine enemies: thou anointest my head with oil; my cup runneth over.

"Surely goodness and mercy shall follow me all the days of my life: and I will dwell in the house of the Lord for ever."

"Alright, already," Jezebel said with a smirk, raising her pistols. "Let's get to the fun part."

The doors creaked, the gunfire simply not enough to stop the wave of undead rushing towards them. The Gatling gun twanged hollowly as it reached the end of its belt, and as the door creaked again and again, more rhythmically, Sereno leapt down from the tower, his borrowed monkish garb billowing in the moonlight as he landed besides them.

The gate burst, and the dead poured through. Holyoak was glad to see that their defense had been effective: Their enemies had to crawl over a mountain of corpses in the doorway.

It was mostly vampires of a certain age and power that had made it this far. He saw silver spurs and ten-gallon hats, gowns of faded finery and glittering jewels, powdered wigs filthy with dirt and age, great sombreros and handlebar moustaches, chaps and boots, and serapes and Stetsons.

He waited until they were close enough to smell, his feet braced and the stock of the shotgun in the crook of his arm. He fired one barrel, sending creatures into the dirt, some killed outright, other scratching out their eyes or clawing at their chests in pain. When the confusion cleared and another wave moved towards him, he fired again into the smoke, letting the blessed splinters do their work.

With a yell and a lilting giggle, Jezebel disappeared into the fray, both guns blazing as Holyoak reloaded the shotgun and slung it into the holster on his back. He quickly surveyed the carnage. Some of the monks were dead or dying, but that was unfortunately to be expected. The line was holding better than he had imagined it would, and some of the brothers were actually doing a god job.

Mostly out of ammo, the monks were coming down from the walls, led by the portly Brother Rodrigo who seemed to have taken a leadership role upon himself. He was deftly reloading his revolver without looking as he barked positions to his brothers, and with a skill and speed that made Holyoak wonder about his former life.

There was a change in the air. Holyoak could feel it as he cut his way through with the machete. The vampires had planned on getting in, murdering some helpless monks and getting out with their bloody prize. Now they were gearing up to fight in earnest, finding strategies, and ganging up on the strongest of them.

Brother Francisco was making admirable use of the simple fighting techniques Sereno had taught him, using his pointed staff to block, slash and pierce the flesh of any bloodsucker that got close enough, but Holyoak saw him being overwhelmed by two strong old *vaqueros* and fired twice from the Colt in his left hand with pinpoint accuracy, putting them down before Francisco even perceived what danger he was in.

Sereno was a whirlwind of fists and kicking blows that shattered the brittle skin and bones of the vampire horde, but Holyoak saw a crafty female creep up from behind him while he tangled with her mate, and fired another deadly shot between her eyes. He was using his bullets well but he would have to—he's equipped himself last, with just enough silver to fill both guns.

Holyoak saw Rodrigo go down with a cut throat, heard Jezebel's cries go from gleeful to genuinely angry, and saw

Sereno bleeding from all over his body, shaking off attackers that latched onto his arms and legs with their teeth.

"At last!" Francisco declared. "He is ready to confess!" He bolted for the church, somehow darting around multiple attackers. Holyoak was aware suddenly of the enormity of the army of undead assailing the compound. But he knew that his suspicions were accurate. The young abbot had been glamoured by the monster beneath them. No matter what was happening here in the courtyard, he would have to follow.

He ran at his best clip, but the abbot was faster and was already in the church. He ran past a red mist and heard cries of joyful murder from a feminine throat. Jezebel, apparently confident at going unnoticed in the chaos, had revealed her demon nature, and the silhouette in the fire-lit cloud was no longer pleasing, with wild joints and a too-wide jaw. Holyoak looked away, narrowly dodging splatters of blood and blackened globs of gore that showered the courtyard dirt from the haze.

There were three bullets left in the Colt he held. Knowing he might need every second, he switched guns on the steps. In the church itself, he glided past the altar and down the stairs into the dungeon, machete above his head and Colt brandished before him, as if either would have done any good.

"Reverend!" Francisco shouted as he entered.

"Where is mercy now?" the monster said pitifully, yet Holyoak sensed the mockery in his tone. "I do repent, and yet I do despair. Hell strives with grace for conquest in my breast. What shall I do to shun the snares of death?"

"I told you." Francisco said, animated with joy. "He is ready to repent and confess! He doesn't need to be destroyed, he can be such a force for good! He can teach us so much! An eyewitness to Christ!"

Holyoak knew it was no use arguing with someone who'd been glamoured by a vampire. The spell was too deeply rooted in one's own hopes, fears, and insecurities.

"And what about faith, brother?" Holyoak asked, moving just a little bit closer. He hadn't got the hang of the mechanism that controlled the stake-tipped pendulum above them, but could recognize that the placement of the knobs was different. Presumably, Francisco had disabled it.

"We won't need faith anymore, reverend. We will have proof."

"Funny thing about faith and doubt," Holyoak said, again inching closer. "I've seen people go to hell and back and doubt the existence of the Devil, I've seen science ignore spirit and religion ignore fact. I admit, it was a puzzle to me too that anyone, no matter how wicked, could have been in the Lord's presence and still choose evil, but the fact is that even the Good Book is full of just such folks.

"So he heard Jesus speak. A lot of people hear the Word and don't take it into their hearts. A lot of people *preach* the Word and don't believe it if their actions say anything."

Francisco was shaking his head, as if waking up from a dream, he had taken a step back but was still in the creature's reach.

"There is one other thing that bothers me though," he continued, directing his words now to the old vampire. "Just what were you doing living with those lepers anyway?"

The monster smiled hideously.

"Feeding."

Francisco tried to back away, but the vampire snapped the heavy chains of silver around his body as though they were plastic, seizing the screaming monk and pulling him towards his maw.

Holyoak fired, lodging a silver bullet squarely in the creature's wrist. The monk clattered on the floor and immediately obeyed Holyoak's command:

"Run! Get outta here!"

The creature bounded at him, and though squat and small-legged closed the gap fast. Holyoak fired the five remaining bullets in the Colt at it point-blank and though blood trickled from its wounds, it merely stopped, anxious to attack, wary of the blessed steel that Holyoak wielded in the other hand.

The creature growled when Holyoak cut his way past him, having to let go of the machete now lodged halfway through its wrist. Holyoak dove for the console, the vampire's teeth and hands narrowly missing him as he followed behind. He knew nothing about its workings, no idea which knob to pull or how long the wooden point would take to fall. But he would leave that to God.

He would not doubt.

He reached for the knob that seemed most likely, the one in red, emblazoned with a golden cross. He turned, drawing the other Colt 45 and pressing the trigger twice in rapid succession. Just enough to sweep the thing off its feet and into the path of the deadly hammer swinging down, the huge stake bursting through his enormous chest and spraying Holyoak—and much of the room—with blackened blood.

The creature's weight was such that it merely slid back, balancing the pendulum near the center of its arc.

"You have not won," it said coldly, blood dripping from its mouth into its matted beard. "That was the first lesson I learned from humans. Be it a colony of lepers, or the poor crossing your borders, the slave pits or Rome, or"—it licked its lips obscenely—"of Georgia: my kind will always thrive because there will always be people you would rather not see."

Holyoak picked himself up and came closer.

"Could there be mercy for a creature like me?"

"Yes," Holyoak said, not with doubt, but with caution.

"Then in your prayers…" The vampire clutched at Holyoak's shirt, pulling him close enough to smell the decay on its breath. "…tell your God that he has failed. I reject it."

"Tell him yourself," Holyoak said, navigating the barrel of the Colt beneath the creature's chin. He fired his last silver bullet, and the monster dropped him. He retrieved the machete from its wrist, and severed it head in three ragged blows, blood spurting in all directions from its leathery neck.

The earth began to rumble, and Holyoak was stricken with a panicked need to get out of that space. He ran for the door, up the stairs and back out into the courtyard, only remembering halfway that this really wasn't over—they were still under attack, fighting a battle that they would probably lose.

He emerged from the church into the din of combat. They were, miraculously, still holding their own but by a hair's breadth. Suddenly he lost his footing, as the ground rippled and quaked around the church, the roof of which blew off in a cascade of blue flame. The vampires were more stunned by this then the monks, and many of them burst into the same fire, their skin cracking and bubbling like glass. The numbers were more even now, and the tide of battle turned again. Many of the vampires, robbed of the prize and unsure of their fate began to run away.

A great burst of power erupted from the church again, this time shaped like an expanding dome. Any vampire that it touched was instantly burned down to a withered stack of ash and bone, and they were fleeing in earnest now. The wave dissipated just outside the walls, merely burning and scarring the undead that it touched. Holyoak retrieved the shotgun from its holster on his back, Sereno cracked his neck with a stake in either hand, and both, with Jezebel—

caked from head to toe in gore and blood—pursued the rest outside.

The sun was rising and the creatures were trying to go to ground. Holyoak emptied his shotgun into the backs of two pale skinned old cowboys as they ran bowlegged for cover. Jezebel reached for the head of a yellow-skinned *señorita* that had gotten the rest of her body underground and merely twisted it off with a laugh, and Sereno, keenly attuned to the soil, went to the places where some had already concealed themselves and drove the stakes into their hearts.

Though out of silver, Holyoak was still well equipped with his makeshift vampire-shot, and they continued, fanning out from the compound and mopping up the rest of the mess. Meanwhile the monks staked and salted any remains inside the walls, including with sadness, the bodies of their brethren, preparing a great bonfire which would be fed with corpses for the rest of the day and probably the night.

Holyoak limped inside to his cell. Now it would be time for a bath and the sweet release of sleep.

VI

THE SUN rose on a new day. The walls of the monastery compound were damaged, the gates broken, and the church nearly destroyed. But the ashes had been swept away and the blood shoveled over. The monks were already at work on repairs. In a month it would be as if nothing had happened at all.

Holyoak had dreaded going back down into that dungeon, but also trusted that God would have urged him in his heart to go sooner if something had been amiss. Nothing remained of their ancient enemy but a flash of discoloration where his body had been when it released its awesome powers.

The reverend sat outside now, enjoying a breakfast of coffee and cigarettes with the great wrestler and the young abbot. Sereno's wounds had healed, since the vampires that had bitten him were all dead., but the monks had dressed him in bandages soaked in holy water, just to be safe.

"Where will you go now?" Brother Francisco asked.

"Back to Mexico City," Sereno said. "I'm late for a movie."

"What'll you tell them about the delay?" Holyoak grinned.

"Most likely, something near the truth." Sereno said, his smile flawless behind the mask. "They never believe me but it's always good publicity."

"And you?" Francisco asked.

"I don't know," Holyoak said coolly, savoring the bitterness of coffee and smoke. "I'll have to see what the Lord has planned."

"I wish I had your faith," the young abbot said sincerely.

"Don't be ashamed to doubt, brother," Holyoak said thoughtfully, looking at the mountains around them. "That's the shadow in the valley, I think: doubt. Doubt always finds a way. Faith you have to work at, you have to choose it every day. And really it's doubt that makes it strong." Holyoak looked the young abbot in the eye. "I wish I had *your* faith. The Lord isn't shy about telling me what he wants. You have to guess." He smiled warmly and they laughed at this together, but it was time to go.

He stood up, and Francisco took his hand in both of his. "Keep the faith then, Brother Xavier."

Holyoak nodded, and looked at Sereno, who merely raised his hand.

"The studio is sending a car."

"'Til we cross path again, then." Holyoak extended his hand, and they shook firmly.

Then he moved out to the courtyard where the Bel Air was parked.

"Got a light?" Jezebel sat on a bench behind one of the outlying buildings, a cigarette between her fingers. She was still dressed as a nun—in her slightly off high-heels. Holyoak reached into his coat and produced a lighter.

"After what I saw last night, I'm gonna make believe that you actually need one of these to start a fire."

"You saw that, huh?" she asked, swinging a long leg playfully and giving him a shrug that made her bosom bounce enticingly. "A girl's gotta eat."

He lit her cigarette. He'd known what she was, but even now, having *seen* what she was, being so close to her was a thrill.

"Give a girl a ride?" she asked with a wink. "Just to the next service station?"

"Not this time. I don't think the roads we're taking line up—or end in the same place."

"Well maybe they'll cross again."

"Maybe," Holyoak smiled, mostly to himself.

"I guess I could just stick around here for a while then," she said, examining her manicure coyly. "It could be a lot of fun."

"Go easy on them, okay," Holyoak said, his smile widening. "They don't know what they're getting into."

"Good luck, Reverend," she said with a wave as he walked away. "And make sure you listen to the radio. You never know what you might hear."

Holyoak drove the winding road from the monastery for what felt like a long time, alone in the silence of the car. At last he came to the fork that would lead him back to what he was now thinking of as home. He knew in his heart when he left that he probably wouldn't be returning, but now he felt the horrible burden on his heart telling him to keep moving on.

To his left was the road that would take him to the freeway going North and East, where Dawn was waiting for him—to rest, happiness, even love.

The road to the right would take him West, through paths unknown. There waited fire, chaos, rivers of blood—and salvation.

"At least let me know, Lord, when my work is done. Give me a sign and make it plain."

But the only answer was the silent command in his heart: "Go."

He turned right, into the setting sun, and switched the radio on.

For today at least, he would keep the faith.